Coffeedreamz Ink, LLC

I0664992

Caramel's Sunday

By

Yolonda D. Coleman

CARAMEL'S SUNDAY

Copyright © 2014 by Coffeedreamz Ink, LLC. Printed and bound in the United States of America. All Rights reserved. No part of this book may be reproduced or transmitted in any form or by any electronic or mechanical means including photocopy, recording, or any information storage and retrieval systems without permission in writing from the publisher or except in the case of brief quotations in reviews or articles. Any unauthorized act in relation to this publication may be liable for criminal prosecution and civil claims and damages.

Cover Design by

Barron Steward
www.barronsteward.com

For booking information visit
www.yolondacoleman.com.

Caramel's Sunday is a work of fiction inspired by research, family history, and experience. The characters, most places, and most events are products of the author's imagination or used fictitiously.

ISBN: 978-0-9800071-3-8

To order additional copies, please visit
www.amazon.com Keyword: Yolonda D. Coleman

Editorial Team

Treesa Elam-Respass, Letessa Jackson, Ericka Jeter, Rebecca Jones, Montreal McMorris, and Carissa L. Schorback

The Dedication

I dedicate this book to my husband, Sir Dreck Body, my sister-friend, Treesa Elam-Respass, and my grandpa, Eddie D. Coleman.

Sir Dreck, thanks for your patience. In the final hours of this book, you let me disappear into my literary world with complete support.

Treesa, thanks for never letting me give up on this project. Thank you for always cheering me on when my dream tank was empty. Thank you for your ministry in my life.

Grandpa, you first introduced me to God. I am blessed to know the love of the Lord through your ministry. Because of Him, my dreams never sleep.

The Revelation

Life can cause you to change your heart time and time again; it can cause you to lose focus of the goal. The road is weary and lonesome. This is what happens when you have a dream. If you look at Joseph, his dream lead him to be hated upon, jailed, and isolated for what God revealed to him, but it also promoted him and blessed him. There was a period of pain, but the pain was temporary and part of the process.

Others may not always agree with your vision, they may not believe in your vision, and they will doubt your ability to fulfill your vision even if they will benefit from it; but that's ok. It's not the dream and vision God gave to them; it's yours. Do not allow life to distract you. You can't afford to lose focus or not believe in the vision. Have a "Finding Nemo" moment. Tell yourself, "Keep swimming, just keep swimming, just keep swimming..."

-Ideana Nikki Glenn
High Point, NC

Somebody Testify

Caramel's Sunday will make you remember your youth and personal development.

-Van Johnson III, Esq., MA

"*Caramel's Sunday* is a story many can relate to when contemplating the life choices they will be making or have already made."

-Leslie Jones, GA

"There is no way you can read this and not feel some sense of pride or not feel like the characters could be you. Like Coleman's previous two books, *Caramel's Sunday* makes you want to keep turning the pages."

-Kwane Reed, VA

"*Caramel's Sunday* is an inspiration, easy to read, and just a great story."

-Roxanne Fails, MD

"I believe *Caramel's Sunday* will motivate people to follow their dreams but also to dig deep within their hearts and search for their truest desires.

-Cassandra Williams, IL

"*Caramel's Sunday* is very captivating and gave me a great feeling of nostalgia."

-Montreal McMorris, D.C.

CARAMEL'S SUNDAY

SLEEP STAGE 1
"Between Being Awake and Falling Asleep"

When we sleep well, we wake up feeling refreshed and alert for our daily activities. Sleep affects how we look, feel and perform on a daily basis, and can have a major impact on our overall quality of life.

To get the most out of our sleep, both quantity and quality are important...If sleep is cut short, the body doesn't have time to complete all of the phases needed for muscle repair, memory consolidation, and release of hormones regulating growth and appetite. Then we wake up less prepared to concentrate, make decisions, or engage fully in school and social activities.
-The National Sleep Foundation

This first stage of sleep is called the "introduction into sleep." It is frequently observed by watching someone's head nod when they are listening to a dull lecture. This stage is marked by a slowing down of brain activity and a beginning of muscle relaxation. You can be easily awoken from this stage, which is why you find yourself jumping awake for seemingly no reason.
-The Center of Sound Sleep

CARAMEL'S SUNDAY

JPEG 001
Inheriting the Dream

"Researchers do not fully understand REM sleep and dreaming. They know it is important in the creation of long-term memories. If a person's REM sleep is disrupted, the next sleep cycle does not follow the normal order, but often goes directly to REM sleep until the previous night's lost REM time is made up."

-Dr. Mark Stibich

CARAMEL'S SUNDAY

Everything I know about sex and relationships I learned from Salt-N-Pepa. Although I was only nine when *Hot, Cool, & Vicious* dropped, I learned that most men were *tramps.* I had no clue what a tramp was, but I knew it was bad. So I kept my eyes on my studies and my legs closed.

By eighth grade, my breasts bloomed and the boys wanted to *talk about sex*; however I remembered the girl in Salt-N-Pepa's video who was "mad and sad and feeling bad, thinking about things that she never had." Because I didn't want to be her, I stayed off the promiscuous teen track.

My *mic* was a camera, canvas, and paint brush in high school. Therefore, I really didn't have time for much outside of school and art club. I was a bit of a recluse. Aren't most artists? Boring, my life was not. I lived and loved through the adventures of others who lived inside my 35mm camera.

The most important lesson I learned from the lyrics of Cheryl James and Sandy Denton was that sex didn't make love; only seasoned love produced healthy offspring. Love was something very abstract for me. Aside from the southern affection of my friends and family, the only tangible manifestation of love was in the works I created. I could touch what I created. I saw the joy my work brought to the lives of others.

If scientists believe memories become permanent at age three, then the memory of love I knew died five years after the marking point. Both of my parents were murdered when I was eight years old. I watched them die in my camera. In their deaths, I learned to live.

My art fueled me. It became my air. Creating art allowed my mother's life to sing and live on. She taught me how to illustrate. We scribbled on napkins and drew on my plain bedroom wallpaper with crayons. The bubbles from my bath were more than spherical soap suds. They were used to create a mask for me and one for her. I washed, played, and created in the bathroom. Breakfast always had a smile. Blueberries were the eyes of my pancakes. Orange slices kissed me each Saturday morning. Shredded hash browns mimicked my long hair with ketchup as red highlights.

Whenever I snap photos, I am reminded of the first time I learned about light and lenses from my daddy. Morning and evening were the same to me. Filters made the sunset look like morning and the sunrise look like evening. The sky was a rainbow paint splash. Daddy could make a country road look like a city skyline from the street lights. He was amazing.

What I know of my parents was enough for me to pursue my dreams even in the face of death. They both had stable jobs. Dad was a mechanic. Mom was a secretary at my elementary school in Garysburg, North Carolina. They both went to work happy but came home even more zealous to immerse themselves in their hobbies. I was caught in the middle of two romantic artists who never fulfilled their life's passion because responsibilities and life itself happened.

I often heard my aunts and uncles tell my mom that she had to stop living in the clouds because her art wasn't going to feed the family. I heard my uncles tell my dad that being a photographer was not a real job.

"A man needs ta' provide fo' his family," Uncle Leonard encouraged strongly.

Ironically, Mom and Dad left me in the care of my very concerned aunties and uncles--their siblings. They were to rear and encourage me into my destiny in the absence of my parents. Part of that rearing included me going to school and renting my time out by getting a job. My plan was to follow my heart's desire and build a career off my passion. Needless to say, my plan was pretty unpopular. I had to make a believer out of a lot of people whose idea of success included making other people wealthy. I had to make a believer of those who thought dreams were only moving pictures for us to view while sleeping.

While my dream requires only that I participate in life, some close members in my circle believe that by my 30th birthday, I should be walking down an aisle in a white dress holding the freshest flowers money could buy. Instead, I'd be more inclined to catch a glimpse of a bride and her groom at an altar than standing in front of one myself.

Throughout my journey, I had to be reminded of my grandfather's words to me when I turned 18.

"Caramel, I don't care what happens in life; you keep your mind fixed on God and yo' dreams 'til no mo' breath is in you," he said.

"I promise, Gramps. I promise."

The legacies of my parents and Gramps would live through my work. Along the journey, I was certain I would tickle my aunties and acquire a husband. He would, however, have to chase me down and physically pry my lenses open for me to see love before my flower blossomed and opened for him. I stood alone in my journey, but it was one I was willing to travel.

CARAMEL'S SUNDAY

SLEEP STAGE 2
Waking Up to Dream

A relaxation takes over the body to prepare for the dreams that are coming.

-The Center for Sound Sleep

JPEG 002
A Snapshot of the Future

"People can use their most treasured desires to escape from other things. The intent is great but may come with a cost if they aren't balanced."

-LaShaun Warren
Bowie, Maryland

CARAMEL'S SUNDAY

I drive out of Earth's mouth every Wednesday at 6:00 a.m. to catch a glimpse of the sun's eyes opening. Trees along Route 210 in Fort Washington, Maryland are like arms ushering me into a new day. The road, with its paved blacktop and sporadic white lines, keeps me in my lane and keeps me from worrying about what others are doing in the fast lanes of life. I have a quick commute to Union Station for the 7:30 a.m. train to New York City; I take the trip to shop my portfolio to advertising agencies for freelance work. I would later discover my sojourn north was not in vain. I was planting seeds.

My forever passenger is my camera. In a flash, I get to capture life happening. I get to see the smiles of those who desire to be my subject for a few snapshots. Buildings pose while birds fly and clouds glide across the sky just to be in photographs. Life is an advertisement that I get to share with the world.

Some find their lives are defined by images that tell them how to live and whom to follow. I learned, over time, to follow my own images after three events helped me decide which images to emulate and which to claim as uniquely mine. I followed the crowd three days out of my life. The first day was in high school when I tried to fit in with the cool girls.

My cousin, Dolly, usually spent her last week of summer with me in North Carolina. School started later for her than it did for me. At the time, she and her family lived in Washington, D.C. Living in the city was very cool to me; Dolly was a cool girl, so I got some of what I thought was coolness from her. Dolly was able to do things a little earlier than I. She could wear makeup and hang out with friends past the illumination of the street lights at age 15. Because I wasn't allowed to wear makeup until I was 16, I tried to buck the rules of the house and snuck a tube of Cousin Dolly's lipstick in my pocket the night before my first day of 10th grade. She would barely notice because her collection of cosmetics in her Caboodle makeup case was scattered. I just grabbed what felt right.

The sun was shining and students gleefully hopped out of their cars or off the county bus. We all waltzed in the building as if summer never began or ended. It was a happy August morning. On past first-days, I'd look like any ordinary student coming through the front doors. There was nothing special or breathtaking about my appearance prior to 1991.

Khakis, a printed shirt, and sandals were my usual attire. My hair would be held together with a stylish scünci, but that was about as bold and beautiful as I would get. On this beautiful Monday morning, however, I wore black stretch stirrup pants with a long, slightly-fitted yellow shirt that was tied at the left corner in a knot. Cousin Dolly crimped my hair but left my bang straight in the front. Few people saw me with my hair down. I didn't want to give them all that red at once. I turned a few heads as if I were the new girl in school.

Just before homeroom, I went into the restroom to apply the lipstick and had the bright idea to smear a little over my eyelids. I didn't have eye shadow and thought that lipstick would do the same thing--give my eyes some color as it did my lips.

I pranced out of the restroom as fresh as a breeze and bumped into Shelly Royal, the most admired girl in school. Shelly was with her crew. We called her the Queen G, the Queen of Gaston High. Shelly was as smart as she was stylish. Unlike most popular girls, she wasn't purposefully malicious with her comments. She stopped and stared at me for a minute. Then she spoke.

"Hi, Caramel! I see you've brightened up a little since last school year."

"Hey, Shelly. I guess I have," I agreed while continuing my stroll down the hall feeling quite confident and accepted at the same time. Tenth grade was going to be remarkable.

I entered homeroom, which combined all grade levels. I sat next to Solomon, my best friend; he was a senior.

"I like your new look, Mel," he said.

"Thanks. You don't look so bad yourself, Sol!" I said.

"Are you kissing the rainbow?" Solomon asked. I was puzzled.

Solomon was known for cracking jokes, but I couldn't quite catch the punch line this time. Solomon pointed to the glass cabinet that held the supplies for class just behind me. I stood and looked at a reflection that was quite different from the one I had left in the mirror of the restroom. One of my eye lids was green, one was blue, and the shade on my lips had turned from rouge to purple. My face looked like a bag of Skittles. I pulled the lipstick out of my purse; it was maroon, just as I had remembered. The color morphed. I looked on the bottom of the tube to find the words *Mood Lips with VitaE*. It was makeup that changes color with the pH level in the user's skin.

CARAMEL'S SUNDAY

Solomon couldn't stop laughing. Tears streamed out of his eyes. He wound up getting put out of homeroom after the attendance clerk called roll because his cackling annoyed our teacher. Some old, dead theorist said our childhood experiences shape our adult lives; therefore, I'm more partial to clear lip gloss these days. If I ever wear a color, it's pretty rare. I'd have to be in a photo shoot instead of shooting a photo.

The next episode of *Keeping up with the Joneses* came during my junior year of college. I was officially dating Solomon. Best friends make the best lovers. Right? Well, my girlfriends at St. Augustine's College thought it would be a nice change for me wear three-inch pumps one Friday night Solomon came to take me out. I fought them on the makeup. It just wasn't happening. Makeup and I still had beef. One of those girlfriends, ironically, was Shelly. She and I became friends once she realized she was the only one in her crew who had ambitions and wanted to go college instead of impressing boys all her life. Shelly had style; I trusted her.

"Just put one foot in front of the other, Mel!" Shelly yelled from the other end of the dorm hallway.

My trip down the imaginary catwalk went well in Suber Hall. I worked my walk as if *Doin' It* by LL Cool J was my theme music. I was standing as tall as the Brooklyn Bridge while New York City blinked lights for queens hailing from the Bronx. I was fly. That's what my New York City classmate told me.

Solomon picked me up on time, as usual. Because his grin was not followed by laughter, I was confident he liked my upgrade. The closer Solomon moved toward me, the shorter he became. If the shoes were two inches shorter, we would have been the same height. I'm 5'10" without the shoes. He's 6'. I towered above him. Making light of an embarrassing moment, Solomon just smiled, but I imagined him thinking, "Make room for Big Bird."

I glanced at Shelly. She cupped her mouth and whispered, "Sorry," to me just before Solomon and I started walking out of the door.

I made it safely to the car and into the restaurant. I'm sure Solomon and I looked like an odd couple, but the maître d' and staff kept welcoming us with warm smiles on their faces without making us feel uncomfortable. I sat down most of the evening. I didn't want to risk falling down or bumping into anyone while trying to find my balance. I even held my bladder until it was time to go. Nothing ruins an evening like falling into a public toilet. After I freshened up, I had a new burst of energy and wanted to go dancing.

"Are you sure, my Amazon queen?" Solomon asked with a smirk looking up at me while walking down the stairs to the garage.

"I'm positively..."

In mid-response, I lost balance because the heel of my shoe got caught in a groove, and I tumbled down plastic-covered steps. My purse broke my fall and protected my face. Something that felt like a rock was in the foot of my panty hose. A closer look revealed that one of my toenail tips broke off. Surprisingly, it did not hurt, but the toe looked like a man with a receding hairline. The whole episode was funny later in the night. I came to the revelation that I was made to wear shoes with no more than a one-inch lift. It was all the height I needed.

The last train toward Caramel's Way happened in 2000. I often get crossed looks when I talk about the last day I decided to turn my back on society's thoughts of my decisions.

One little detail about Solomon that is worth mentioning is that he comes from an affluent family. Solomon Montgomery Brooks is the great-grandson of Vincent Wellington Brooks, Sr., of Brooks Food, Inc., the largest food distributor along the Atlantic coast for hotels and schools. Solomon's family had old money. It was so old that even if the company went bankrupt, they'd still have millions in liquid assets. Although he wasn't a direct heir to the food empire, his name certainly carried with it a heavy reputation.

Solomon's father, Robert Stanley Brooks, wanted to tap into commercial real estate along Interstate 95-- malls, grocery stores, highway restaurants, and so forth. He decided to move to Garysburg, North Carolina. Our small town was just a few miles from Roanoke Rapids, North Carolina, a major city on the rise that would prove later to be a frequent stop for travelers heading into the Carolinas on I-95. It didn't hurt to have a big name in a small town. The first major venture was opening a popular chopped barbecue joint called Stan's BBQ. It drew patrons from all around. The Brooks family built a fortune off its success and continued to flourish from there.

In the summer before my senior year at St. Augustine's, I took some time off to follow my dream as an artist and photographer. Okay, let me be truthful. I dropped out of school for a few years with every intention of returning. I was just ready to get to work. The passion for my art was a burning desire that could only be cooled by doing it more often. Solomon was in the five-year M.B.A. program at Dukem University. Shortly after finishing his degree, he proposed. I said yes, of course, and we became the talk of North Hampton County in North Carolina. I was 21 years old, and according to my aunts, I was the perfect age to start a family and young enough not to be tainted by the world.

Solomon's father wasn't sold on the idea of us getting married. He thought I was a gold digger. His mother, on the other hand, enjoyed seeing her son happy. She particularly liked the fact that I was an artist. Mama Montgomery was an art collector, so her birthday and Christmas presents included originals from me to her.

Although there was some pressure for us to plan the wedding right away, Solomon wanted to see the rest of the world and find his place in it without the help of his family's name. I agreed. Before we could get anyone's permission to chart the course of our lives, we moved to New York City to find our way.

Solomon was in search of a lucrative career in the music industry, and I wanted to be a photographer for an advertising agency. It didn't take Solomon long to mix and mingle with the super producers who smacked a hit song into existence with their eyes closed. Solomon had what the executives wanted. Sales and marketing were a part of Solomon's genetic design. After a few industry parties, wining and dining label executives Solomon had a ticket to success.

While others had to start at the bottom--passing out promotional postcards and so forth--Solomon became VIP at the clubs on his own merit. He was put on the management and marketing team for mega stars like Tres Chain E., J9, Waterfront, and Sam'One. He helped to elevate their careers even further in less than six months, and like Puffy, he wasn't going to stop. He was a natural manager.

When I decided that the Big Apple was too much for a country girl without a college degree, I called Dolly and asked if I could stay with her until I got my head together. She barely occupied her apartment. At the time, Dolly was teaching. Her routine included making a bee-line straight to her boyfriend's house after work. I gave her a few dollars I made from freelance gigs in order to take care of my portion of rent. I used the other half for classes that I could credit toward my program at St. Augustine's. I just needed to keep my feet wet in the world of academia so I wouldn't be too far behind.

CARAMEL'S SUNDAY

Solomon and I took turns visiting each other every other weekend. By the second year of our long distance relationship, unwanted stress came from a long line of women who married their best friends and first loves to set a date for the wedding; my aunts overwhelmed me. The more I thought of getting married the more I realized I wasn't really ready for all that glitters or the gold in Solomon's world of music just yet. I wanted to make my own mark before I became barefoot and pregnant sitting in the lap of his luxury. I had to carry my own weight.

When the lifestyles of the rich and famous became more and more attractive and the dream became bigger than Solomon, I saw a pattern that I didn't want to get caught up in. The web of greed and self-service were taking a toll on our relationship. As a result, I started heading for the border. No, I don't mean Taco Bell.

I remember the day I called it quits as clear as the crystal glasses we received as an engagement present. Solomon and I were both in D.C. for Howard University's homecoming weekend. He was promoting his new artists who were performing at various night clubs. I was building my portfolio for a project I called *On the Shoulders They Stand: A Real Homecoming*. While Solomon concentrated on the entertainment, I wanted to capture the alumni who so proudly boast about their alma mater while writing checks as they check on their investments.

I met Solomon at Ben's Chili Bowl, a novelty diner on U Street in D.C. I was wearing a pair of blue jeans and a white hoodie with a rhinestone camera on it. I walked in wearing my Princess sneakers where my feet comfortably rested in my blue and white ball socks; however, Solomon looked at me as if I stepped on the scene in onesie pajamas and a head full of sponge rollers. My attire might not have come close to his high-end standard, but I was doing my *thang* in my way.

"Why are you dressed like that, Mel?" he asked.

"Dressed like what, Sol?" I asked with a raised eyebrow.

Solomon paused before speaking as he rubbed his chin between his right index finger and thumb; then he let out what seemed to be a harmless laugh as he sized me up.

"Mel, we're in the middle of one of the biggest social events of the season in D.C. I know you have something more stylish than a pair of jeans and a sweatshirt. You never know who might see me," he said.

CARAMEL'S SUNDAY

This was not the first time Solomon was embarrassed by my relaxed look. While we both had the same affection for each other privately, he was more concerned about his public image than I cared about mine. My work required me to be in the background while he lived to be in the foreground. There are times I have to dress professionally, but being on U Street in the middle of the afternoon was not one of them.

Solomon reached in his back pocket and pulled out his wallet. He handed me $600 and a key to his hotel room at the Grand Hyatt.

"Mel, take this and buy something from the boutique near the hotel," he said.

I stared at him with a smile, while pondering, *He's kidding right?* He also reminded me to *accessorize.* I continued to smile and nod...smile and nod.

"I have a meeting with some folks in a few. I shouldn't be longer than two hours, but I'll pick you up as soon as I'm done," Solomon said.

He kissed me on the forehead, pulled out his cell, and started dialing a number while I stood with my empty smile. Please know that I'm no fool. I took the money, and I went shopping. Afterward, I went back to the hotel room, changed into my new designer dress, and put on my new 1-inch pumps. I combed out my hair, added some clear gloss to my lips, set my camera on a tripod to take a picture of myself, and then a picture of the engagement ring inside his suitcase. I emailed the images to Solomon along with a simple note.

Solomon,

Thanks for the shopping spree and a glimpse of our future. Find me when your head is leveled with the dream and not above it.

-Ms. Violet Caramel Moss

I walked out of the Grand Hyatt with a renewed spirit. I used the remaining money to tip the valet in a huge way and went on about my business. Since that day, I started taking more and more courageous steps on my own. Taking that step at 24 years old opened up immediate doors.

While I was shooting pictures for an alumni event at Howard University's Blackburn Center, I ran into a gentleman who owned an art gallery. He was looking for someone to rent space for a month. I'd earn 60% of the revenue I sold and an opportunity to showcase both my artwork and photography at an annual fundraiser. After our initial meeting, he scheduled to set me up right away in a prime location on U Street. Ironically, the gallery was right across the street from Ben's Chili

Bowl. That gig exposed me to other opportunities in D.C., Maryland, and Virginia.

After my seventh show, I was able to rent a condo in Ft. Washington, Maryland, in a live/work space near an affluent neighborhood called Stallion Estates. I lived upstairs and managed the framing store downstairs. The owner let me display some of my work in the store's window. If a customer inquired about it, the owner gave me the green light to sell it and split the cost with him-- 50/50. It seemed that I flourished more as an individual than as a plus-one.

I'm not anti-marriage. I'm not anti-love. I just believe that before I can give my entire heart to another soul, I had to give my heart to my dream, void of the pressures of life to be a person who fits into a mold in front of or behind the scene.

I don't regret the day I took hold of my life and started living for my dream. I do miss my best friend who laughed at my dry jokes or who, when he wasn't being Mr. Show Stopper, allowed me to just *do me* without judgment. His affluence afforded me keys to doors of some of the country's most beautiful places-- the Bayou in New Orleans, the Everglades of Florida, the mountains of Colorado, and the Bay Area in California. We spent countless weekends sitting courtside at NBA games. It didn't matter who played, I just loved basketball. Even with all of those memories, nothing meant more than my peace of mind. I was not willing to barter a piece of myself for wealth.

The absence of a love interest didn't make me lonely. The lack of company of my best friend made me yearn for someone who totally *got me.* Then, in 2004, I started thinking of Solomon when Dolly got engaged to a man she truly adored. I saw the happiness she still had with a booming career and a husband to-be. From my lens, Dolly and Gerald understood how to live life, love each other, and find balance without fatal compromises. They became the personification of love's liberation and love's elevation.

It took one failed previous engagement, losing a baby, and second chances for Dolly to realize much of what my journey would teach me. Even still, I was caught between life's dreams and freedom and love and joy with someone who had a shared vision. That's the one thing my early morning sojourn could never reveal to me. The gaps between the sporadic white lines in the road had to be filled within its framework and in its own time.

JPEG 003
Wake Up. Dream. Make It Happen.
(Circa 2004)

"Women are empowered to do things for their personal edification while upholding traditional values. Caramel highlights some of the issues that courageous women, who step out to do what's best for their own interests, have to deal with."

-Doriannicole Standish
Clinton, Maryland

CARAMEL'S SUNDAY

Click! Flash! Click! Flash! While the getting was good, I got it. I juiced the fruit of opportunity for all it was worth and going back to St. Augustine's was a passing thought when checks with four or more zeros passed through my young fingers. In spite of the new money, I had to stay the course and get on track, learn how to stay in the game, and make everyone who questioned my dreams a liar.

My twenties were good to me. Keeping a low profile and letting my work speak for itself paid off. My artwork and photography are still seen throughout the D.C. Metropolitan area in restaurants, night clubs, and houses with a price tag beyond my imagination, but they were products of a time when the land of milk and honey flowed like a river.

Everyone became a potential client for me--family, friend, and foe. I learned that at Cousin Dolly's graduation ceremony at Hampton in 1998. President William R. Harvey told the graduates, "In life, you'll have temporary friends, temporary enemies, but always maintain permanent interests." So when Cousin Dolly had her post-break-up *Come to Jesus* revelation prior to hooking up with Gerald, she quit teaching and became a real estate agent. We both shared a common interest.

She had vacant houses to sell, and I had artwork to help her sell them. While I'm not aggressive with my business tactics, I do know how to wheel and deal. Networking, according to my aunts, was a big part of my father's modus operandi. If Daddy wanted something, Daddy got it! With that said, I was as professional with my cousin as any other business prospect.

"Dolly, I'm sending my portfolio to your office. I think you'll find some great decoration pieces for your upcoming open house for the Woocley Park listing. Call me when you're finished selecting your top ten," I said on her voicemail.

Two hours later, Dolly and I set up a lunch date to grab a bite to eat and hang two pieces in a property worth almost a million dollars. Little did I know the house would be sold to filmmaker Gregorio Modesto. One of the pieces was mixed art on canvas titled *Heart's Desire.* The basic concept was love in the middle of chaos. In the midst of the gray lines, black dots, and red swirls was a three-dimensional, white heart that appeared to move any time you walked by it. It was hard to ignore, just like the very thing you love. The second piece was called *Capitol Offense.* It was actually a photograph that I finally decided to part with after the break-up with Solomon.

CARAMEL'S SUNDAY

I set up the tripod to capture Solomon and I holding hands just after the sun descended on the Smithsonian grounds. We faced the Capitol. Without intention, the flash captured the shine on my engagement ring. It glimmered along with the lights of the Capitol, which was the focal point of the photograph. Our hands were just at the base of the building.

Gregorio was so inspired that he decided to name his upcoming film *Capital Offense* with the tagline *Love is a Crime*. He paid me to use the image for the movie advertisement and a hefty tip for the inspiration. *Inspiration* couldn't be a line item in his budget; therefore, the $20,000 came out of his pocket. I had to sign a disclosure statement that would prevent me from seeking further royalty payments. I didn't mind because my total profit from the painting and use of image for advertising was more than enough for me put my life into overdrive. Hush money was fine with me. I could make more art.

A few checks from Gregorio encouraged me to start thinking of housing my work in a more permanent space. Owning and operating an art gallery and photography studio came with great responsibility, so I wanted to be smart about my plan. While I had a lot of on the job training from industry pals and family, there was still some unfinished business I had to complete. A college degree was missing from my repertoire of accolades.

After years of the *fake it 'til you make it* head nods and occasional *mm hmm, exactly* routine, I needed to have more under my belt than talent. If I were truly to lead, I had to make good on a promise to finish school. A dream without a solid background and credentials meant nothing. Besides, I'd be more eligible for grants and other professional incentives as a student than a business owner, even If I were a little older than my classmates.

I was able to advocate to the admissions director my interest to re-enroll at St. Augustine's. Even though there were several years between my last semester of matriculation and re-enrollment, my work experience and a strong recommendation letter from North Carolina Senator Ruby Duff helped build a case for me as well. I completed a photo series for the senator to catalog the work she did on Capitol Hill. The commissioned work led to other jobs with congressional members. It didn't hurt that Senator Duff was a supportive alumna of St. Augustine's.

Even with my high-powered connections, my re-admittance to St. Augustine's did not come with a welcome mat or without a commitment to give my time sharing my professional expertise to aspiring visual artists. I asked to meet with the vice provost to secure my space on campus.

Dr. Helen Joppy sat in her chair with authority. A belle with a very refined look and voice to match spoke to me with a classic southern tongue.

"Ms. Moss, with all of your great intentions of matriculating at St. Augustine's College, why should we consider your request for re-admission and still allow you to keep your credits after being gone for so many years?" she asked.

I matched her posture and spoke with the professionalism of a philanthropist who would add to the school's endowment.

"Dr. Joppy, there is but one answer to your question. St. Augustine's College is where I started my education, was groomed to be a leader in a changing world, and I have no intentions of crediting any other university for my success after I receive a degree from St. Augustine's College." With that said, I offered one of Senator Duff's paintings to be auctioned at the next homecoming event. Moments later, I walked out of Dr.

Joppy's office with a course catalog for the upcoming semester.

While I finished my courses in Raleigh, I conducted professional development workshops twice a month pro bono. This gave me public speaking experience and the students an opportunity to have access to resources beyond the school's walls. I also took some business courses to learn how to be a better proprietor when I was able to open my art and photography studio.

Two semesters later, I was the recipient of a college degree. Although I wasn't able to participate in regular commencement exercises, I later served as the guest speaker at a fundraising event for Senator Duff on campus. Dr. Joppy introduced me, for the first time anywhere, as an alumna of St. Augustine's College.

Just as I took the stage, I looked out in the audience to gauge the climate. There were some stuffed shirts, loose skirts, and spouses who looked like they were forced to be in attendance. Beyond the light from the video camera, there was a smiling figure that looked vaguely familiar. I thought I was dreaming because as soon as I saw the person's face, the space where he stood was now empty. My cue to speak into the mic was the fading applause.

CARAMEL'S SUNDAY

My topic for the evening was *People Fund Dreams*. I handled my business, received a lot of favorable murmurs, and smiled on the way to my seat in the audience with pride when I concluded.

When I stepped away from the podium, the maître d' passed me an envelope with my name on it. The seal was still wet. Inside the envelope was a check for $6,792, the exact amount I had saved and used for tuition. It also came with a note.

Ms. Moss,
Congratulations on your degree and your success.
Go build your dreams.
-A Supporter

CARAMEL'S SUNDAY

JPEG 004
On the Red of a Moving Train
(Circa 2005)

The magic of the movies met my lens. Gregorio requested me to be one of the photographers for the premiere of *Capitol Offense*. He had a connection with a high-end fashion magazine called *On the Red*, and they planned to feature some of the photographs from the red carpet in the magazine. If they liked my shots, I'd get paid. If not, it was a great opportunity where I planted seeds.

The movie included some A-list stars and several up-and-coming actors. I didn't care if Boo Boo the Fool was starring. All I was concerned about was getting the best quality shot to be featured in *On the Red*.

The day before the premiere, I met with Gregorio to discuss logistics. While he was rooting for me to have my photos selected, he knew there were others with more experience who would be sharks after prey to have their winning shots in the magazine.

We met at a tapas bar in Virginia. After we greeted each other with the two-cheek kiss, Gregorio shot straight from the hip. Indistinct chatter was all around us, but he zoomed into my eyes with his ocean blue lenses and said, "You only need one shot, Caramel. Make it a good one," he said making the *r* in my name sound like a tiger's growl.

"I'll do you one better and make my shots look as good as your films." I gave him a wink.

While I appeared confident, I was pretty nervous about the gig. This would be the first time I'd have to prove myself in the company of pros and anyone who might be competition. I did have one thing I'm sure very few of them had; I was starving with motivation. I was hungry for a sustainable life through my art. Their zeal probably left them when experience told them they were the best. I never stopped learning.

I had a booming streak of clients who kept the bills paid, but some folks were starting to cut back on spending. There were rumors about a pending dive in the housing and stock markets. I was just a few months shy of 30 and had to get on my hustle even more if the rumors were true. The Great Gatsbys of the world were of the mind-set to spend, spend, and spend. Those who watched finances, told me to save, save, and save.

"The bubble is going to bust wide open. Watch what I tell ya," Uncle James would caution.

I wasn't quite sure what bubble he was referring to, but I didn't want to be affected by it. Not planning or planting seeds would put me behind schedule and not ahead of the game. I took nothing for granted and jumped at a moment's notice when opportunity knocked on my door.

The premiere was a formal event. I knew the perfect dress to wear, and this was the perfect time to accessorize it. I reached into my closet's past for my $200 ensemble compliments of Solomon Brooks. I couldn't bring myself to wear it because of the memory attached to it; therefore, I went with my trusty black slacks and shirt. I would accessorize with some pearls to give my attire a more formal, feminine touch. I called my trendy cousin for assistance.

"Dolly, I have Gregorio's premiere at 8. I need to stop by your place to pick up a few things for my outfit," I said before she had a chance to say no.

"Mel, what am I going to do with you? I'll be home by 5. Where's the venue?" she asked.

"It's at the McGowan Theater inside the National Archives," I said while packing my garment bag with my clothes. I planned to get ready at Dolly's house. I was sure she wouldn't mind.

"Girl, you might as well get dressed over here. Bring your tail on. I have to be in and out when I do get home."

"Already packing, cuz. And what you got going on? Didn't Gregorio send you an invitation?" I asked.

"Gerald and I are going to the Kennedy Center. One of his kids at the community center is playing in the all-city band. It's sort of a big deal," Dolly said.

"I understand. I know how y'all love the kids," I joked.

"You know we do. We're coming to the after-party. Gotta go. See you in a few."

I zipped the garment bag and jumped in my purple Neon.

Dolly's townhouse was in Largo, Maryland. At the top of her game, Dolly could afford more; however, she lived and breathed by the rule: *spend as if you don't have it.* She often lived well below her means even if she could make $5,000 off a property she sold. Dolly was sharp with her cash.

"If the market does crash, at least I'll have affordable housing to rent," she often reminded me.

Like clockwork, Dolly was home at five. I fingered through her jewelry and actually slipped on a pair of her shoes--1-inch heels of course--that were a little more formal than my flats. They were still comfortable. I replaced her insoles with my own. I was glad we wore the same size shoe.

"What's up, Mel?" Gerald yelled from the bottom of the stairs.

"You know me. I'm on my hustle, G!" I yelled back.

"I feel you! Good luck tonight. Dolly told me about your shoot."

"Thanks, cuz-to-be," I said.

Luckily, my hair was low maintenance. I had the wet-and-go texture on account of my mom's side of the family--that's what Aunt Maggs told me. They fit into the *other* category as far as race is concerned. There were so many ethnic backgrounds running through their blood, they just stopped trying to figure out what to call themselves. By the '80s, they just stuck with being colored.

I was dressed in 30 minutes and made my way to the theater. Being early was key. I wanted to be in position before anyone else had a chance to turn on the power button on his or her external flash. When I arrived at the newly renovated McGowan Theater, the crew was just laying down the red carpet and clasping the velvet rope to the pole. My equipment was attached to me; I was just waiting for the lights and the action.

I positioned myself and made nice with the crew. Seeing that I was the only photographer there, I had an advantage.

CARAMEL'S SUNDAY

"Excuse me, ma'am. Do you mind if I set my tripod up while you set up?" I asked a woman who looked like an event coordinator.

"Knock yourself out," she replied after seeing my VIP pass.

I bought a couple of medium-sized construction cones to surround my equipment. This served two purposes. One, I wanted to caution passersby that equipment was in use, and two, I was marking my territory. There were no rules against it, and I took advantage of the space. There was no room for error. There was no room for me to look like an amateur. Professional courtesy required me to share some of the space, but it did not require me to scoot over and give my shots away. What I lacked in magazine experience, I made up with my street logic. The talent would speak for itself.

By 6:45 p.m., people were lining up for their pictures. While I was clicking away, the other photographers were still scrambling with their equipment.

Snap! Wide-angle shot. Snap! Close-up. Snap! Personality photo.

"Smile! You're on the red carpet," I spoke to the subjects of my photos.

CARAMEL'S SUNDAY

There was one guy who seemingly walked the red carpet at least 10 times. He kept showing up in my shots with different women. He was dapper in his suit. He kept posing as if he was on a billboard advertisement. I actually enjoyed watching him smile. His teeth were perfect and his body was built like a statue, strong and powerful, even through his clothes. He caught my eye; I can't lie; however, I had to stay focused.

Gregorio arrived at 7:45 p.m. He gave me his signature pose. Point, wink, and smile. Snap! Wide-angle. Snap! Close-up. Snap! Personality photo. That's when Mr. Man snuck into yet another shot and invited Gregorio to shake his hand. *Who is this dude?* I pondered.

While a few of the other photographers wandered off to get shots of the cast coming out of the limo, I had already positioned myself to shoot from my spot without moving. My lens could go the distance.

"Gregorio," I yelled above the crowd. "Get the cast together for a group shot!"

Gregorio winked at me and whispered, "Good idea." His double *o*-words were strings of melted cheese off a pizza-- gooey and irresistible.

The other photographers heard my suggestion to get the cast on the red. By the time they hustled back to the promotional background, I had already taken 15 shots. Snap! Wide-angle shot. Snap! Close up. Snap! "Have fun with it guys!" Personality shot.

I called it a wrap and allowed my camera to play with candid shots before the movie started.

At 7:59 p.m., I was in the middle of the theater. I only needed a little light to tell the story of the night. Just before the lights dimmed, I caught Gregorio and the male lead, Michaun Richards, leaning over in conversation. Gregorio's purple Armani shirt was in perfect contrast to Michaun's silver and blue Invicta watch. I was able to capture the same bling I had with the photograph Gregorio used for the movie's ad.

I adjusted my shutter and stood real still to catch Rachelle Knox, the lead female in the movie, carefully tossing popcorn into her mouth. Her wrist was adorned with a diamond tennis bracelet. Wouldn't you know it, the same gentleman who kept showing up in my shots from the red carpet sat next to Rachelle. He had his arm around her and whispered something in her ear. She leaned over and I caught a shot of them while he was grasping his designer tie between his fingers and thumb. It was a classic photo of a couple watching a romantic movie.

All of my mission impossible moves were calculated. The other photographers enjoyed the movie, and I continued to be on the grind. I could still play when one memory card was full. I had four SanDisks to prevent any hiccups. I sat down to watch the premiere for the first half before I began to plot my next moves. During that transition, someone whispered in my ear.

"Did you get my good side?"
I almost wet myself from shock. It was Mr. Personality, the pop-up guy in my shots. I didn't know if he was crazy or strategic. I didn't answer at first.

"I'm sorry. I am Jeffrey Banks," he said.

"Hi. I am watching the movie," I said with firmness.

"I like how you work, Ms. Moss." He had my name on his tongue. He had my attention.

"SHHHH!" someone from behind cautioned us that we were too loud.

"Thank you," I whispered hoping to end the conversation.

"Meet me in the lobby," he said and then got up from the seat like a ninja.

CARAMEL'S SUNDAY

The smell of Jeffrey Banks's cologne lingered. It was rich. It was nothing that came from a counter--in front, behind, or on top of it. He was a man forest. He smelled of dark amber, wild cherries, and sandalwood. I wanted to camp out in his neck. I was about to lift my weight from the seat until I heard the photographer in the film say, "Smile for the camera." I was there for a purpose. If Mr. Banks wanted to see me, he'd have to stand in line behind my ambition.

I didn't wait for the credits to set up at the mouth of theater. I made my way to the lobby before the other photographers could adjust themselves after sitting too long. I wanted reaction shots. I wanted the laughter, the smiles, the bewildered looks, and the hand-locked couples gazing into each other's eyes. I could play with the colors of the rainbow when I edited the shots. That was the fun part. Getting the raw footage was the work. While shuffling feet moved quickly, my position had to be exact or I would miss my targets.

I had worked with professional photographers in the past, Roy Lens, Jack Manners, Torrance Pat'Rick, and Josephine Francis. Each told me that out of 100 frames, I'd be lucky to get 10 great shots. I wanted to maximize that number by 30%. My hand was steady and I learned how to become one with my environment a long time ago.

The after-party tested my skills. With so many moving images, lights, and colors, I had to keep up, so, I summoned a childhood moment when I stood on the side of the tracks as a train was coming. It was the day we buried my parents. I was eight. I ran to a place where no one could hear me scream. The three o'clock train that traveled through Garysburg would be my sound booth. I never planned to jump the tracks. Killing myself was nowhere near the pain I felt as a parentless child.

Choo! Choooo! The ground shook. The nails in the tracks vibrated. Choo! Choooo! I maintained my ground despite the blowing of the autumn wind. Choo! Choooo! I was in a daydream and only saw Mom and Daddy close their eyes for the last time when their killer shot them. Choo! Choooo! I was hiding in the candy aisle with Daddy's Pentax camera he handed down to me. Choo! Choooo! No one could see me. No one could hear me. It was the only time in my life that I pressed the button on a camera and it never made a sound. I was still...my picture helped the police capture the man who murdered my parents. Choo! Choooo! They died inside my camera. Choo! Choooo!

CARAMEL'S SUNDAY

I opened my eyes. The moving train was only two feet from my nose. I stood still while I cried aloud with my eyes fixated on the mass larger than life. If I could take on the moving weight of a train, I could take on the weight of anything else that stood before me or behind me. I take pictures of life so that I won't have to concentrate on death, and my circumstances forced me to become more proficient at my craft. I was forced into my work.

It was only when I came home to review my images that I became fully aware of what I captured. Of the 1,500 shots I took that night, Jeffrey Banks appeared in at least 200. The one he planned was in front of a sponsorship banner that bared his name, contact number, and web site--www.yourbank.org. He stood in front of it as I was taking a picture of the woman who stood in front of him. He was my moving train that wouldn't stop. Yet, I didn't purchase a ticket for the ride until a year later.

CARAMEL'S SUNDAY

JPEG 005
Shooting the Breeze

I didn't get the gig with *On the Red*, but I submitted a few shots to the style section of the Washington *Post*. The group picture of the cast made the cut. I had my first photo credit published in a reputable newspaper. It wasn't the *A* section, but it was enough that *On the Red* was prompted to invite me to sit in on a photo shoot for an upcoming issue. The door opened, and I walked through it. The intern-turned-account-executive in the sales department remembered me dropping off my portfolio at another magazine. My name was familiar. That seed blossomed into a flower.

A few visits to the New York office led to a paid apprenticeship. *On the Red* hired me as a freelance photographer for D.C. events and occasionally called me to cover their weekly Wednesday events in New York City. I was paid $75 per hour plus transportation. The economy was booming, and every celebrity and his mama promoted events requiring my photographic services. As a result, I was busy between 2005 and 2006. I banked the checks to build my empire.

The cards in the universe were laying my way since the movie premiere, and I counted every one as a blessing. I wanted everything I envisioned for my future; to get there, I had to plan my steps to move forward in the direction of my dreams. My chips were stacked; I was hungry.

The owner of my condo was ready to sell, and I was in a position to buy. My credit was good and I had a down payment; however, as the world kept turning, I lost my full-time job at the framing shop. The owner went out of business. Things were beginning to get tight, so I used the money I was saving for a home to keep me afloat until I found another job with a steady income. I also had three months to find a new place to live or buy the unit. Uncle James was right, the bubble was about to burst wide open.

With few long-term jobs on the horizon, I got bored and headed to Hains Point in D.C. just to shoot the breeze. I packed a lunch and sat on a blanket near the Potomac River. Facing the Jefferson Memorial, I snapped shots of tourists in the paddle boats, kids learning how to fly kites for the first time, and lovers holding hands. It was a beautiful spring day.

"Is this seat taken?" I heard a voice ask.

I turned to see a face I could never forget. It was Jeffrey Banks in jogging pants, a tank, and sneakers. I was more than correct about his build; Jeffrey was a perfect 10 under his clothes. It was obvious that time was good to him. He did not let himself go at all.

"Mr. Banks," I said and began to stand to my feet to greet him.

"No. Stay seated, I'll come down to you," he said as he joined me on the blanket.

I stared at him with bewildered eyes. It had been more than a year since our first meeting. I was so caught up in my work that I neglected the pictorial invitation to call him. He all but asked me to do so when he stood in the picture next to his business banner at the after-party.

"You do remember my name," he said as he wiped the sweat from his face and arms with a hand towel.

"How could I forget?" I responded.

"...and the number?" he asked.

"I'm sorry. I didn't know your standing in front of your banner was an invitation for me to call. I like a more direct approach, sir," I said with sarcastic eyes.

Jeffrey laughed. I laughed with him. In an effort to remain on task, I started snapping pictures again. Jeffrey was polite and didn't interrupt until I let the camera hang from my neck.

"You jog here often?" I asked.

"Only every afternoon. I need the fresh air. I live just across the water in Alexandria."

"Well, where do you work?" I asked.

"Where I live. Here and there," Jeffrey replied.

"Oh, so you're like Tommy from Martin. You really don't have a job."

"I think you have a picture that says otherwise, Ms. Moss." Touché! He had me.

"You're a banker?" I asked.

"Correction. I am a Banks who holds banks and bankers accountable."

He was a code. I just nodded and smiled. I wasn't sure what he was trying to say. He could have been a mob man for all I knew. I stopped asking questions so I wouldn't end up in the Potomac for knowing too much.

The air was crisp and nature was our symphony. After a few voiceless moments, Jeffrey excused himself, but not before officially asking me out.

"Well, lady, I have to finish up my run and it looks like you have some more shots to get. Because you like the direct approach, I'll be direct. I'd like to take you out. You don't have to answer right away. When you call, I'll know that you have accepted the invitation," he said.

"What if I don't call?" I asked.

"Then, you don't call, and that will be that."

He placed his card in my camera case. I picked it up to glance at it. By the time I looked up, Jeffrey was gone. He left his woodland scent lingering in the wind. All I could do was laugh. He was smooth, but I knew someone who was as smooth or smoother than Mr. Banks. I had to put in a call to Miss E. Peebles.

CARAMEL'S SUNDAY

JPEG 006
How I Met Miss E.

**Sponsorship Provided by
Tina Fernandez**
Have a Cup on T/Organo Gold
www.haveacupont.myorganogold.com

My 60-and-over-club-card-holder friend and I have an interesting relationship. We speak more than we see each other. We're an odd couple. To see us is to turn your head sideways and say, "Um...how'd they become friends?" She's my senior glam sister-friend; she's been married, separated, divorced, remarried, and a widow all to the same man. The experiences armed her with a wealth of advice to share with whomever she comes in contact.

I met her while shooting portraits at an active adult community in southern Maryland. Her community had a family and friends event, and Josephine Francis recommended me for the assignment; she had a prior family commitment and couldn't fit the event in her schedule. Referrals are your friend. While everyone else was dressed casually, the one person who stood out was a crimson star. From head to toe, she was dressed to the nines. She wore a flowing red dress accented with a red sun hat pulled down to the top of her black and red sunglasses. Her feet were wrapped in red open-toed pumps. She hadn't requested a photo, but I couldn't resist the urge to shoot at will.

She noticed me stealing shots of her and began to pose with elegance. When she came closer to me she engaged me in a conversation.

"Well, if you're going to be the paparazzi, you should at least know my name," she said.

Her voice was soft and sweet like the perfume she was wearing. Her skin had barely shown signs of aging, and the sun danced in the creases of her three visible wrinkles. She was as radiant as her afternoon ensemble.

"I'm Elizabeth Louisa Hamilton-Peebles," she extended her hand to greet me.

"I'm sorry, Ma'am. I'm Violet Caramel Moss."

She gave out her entire name, so I returned the favor by giving her mine.

She sized me up a bit. "There's something familiar about you. Call me Miss E.," she invited.

"Alright, Mrs. E..." I was stopped mid-sentence.

"No *r*. Just Miss and the letter *E*."

"Call me Caramel or Mel. I don't have a preference. I answer to both."

"You need to decide who you're going to be and choose so people respect you for who you become. I'm not gonna charge you for that piece of advice."

"Yes, Ma'am...I mean, Miss E."

"Now, what are you doing out here with your young self?" she asked.

"I'm the photographer for today. Did you sign up?"

"Chile, no!

"Well, if you change your mind, I'll make room for you?"

"For what, young lady?" Miss E. asked with a chuckle.

"You just look like you have a story to tell," I said.

"Honey, I do, but you don't look like you want to pay the price to hear it. Now, excuse me, dear," she said.

My mysterious subject walked off and politely moved me to the side with her left red-gloved hand to get to the buffet line. The wind blew ever so slightly, prompting her to use her other hand to hold the hat in place. I stole another shot. She was a classic, timeless image and what I believed to have unforgettable classic stories to share.

I moved on and let Miss E. enjoy the event. I didn't want to be overly ambitious. I always live by the mantra: *Plant the seed and watch it grow*. The *it* is whatever you conceive.

CARAMEL'S SUNDAY

The portrait sessions began at 3:00 p.m., so I arrived an hour early to set up. The event coordinator scheduled the families ahead of time. The list was waiting for me in the community center. I perused the list to become familiar with the residents' names. All were pre-printed except one. At the bottom was Miss E. The ink was still fresh where she signed her name with a smiley face.

I had a break between my last five sessions, so I decided to grab a bite to eat. The neighborhood association gave me a complimentary meal. I grabbed my tray of standard barbecue fare: one hot dog, one burger, potato salad, dessert, and a canned beverage. I found an empty picnic table in the shade and made my way to it.

I was so hungry I don't remember how many bites it took me to devour the hot dog. Before I finished my burger, Miss E. joined me with a frozen fruit bar in hand.

"Is this seat taken?" she asked.

"No, ma'am, it's not. Please..." I offered her the seat across from me.

Before I could begin my inquiry, Miss E. just started to share.

"My children are grown. One died at birth. I don't have any grandchildren. My son is a career chaser and my daughter dedicates her life to living abroad. My husband is gone to glory. Most people think the *E* in Miss E. stands for Elizabeth, but it s for ebullient," she said with an upward hand motion.

I didn't know what to say about her family without saying the wrong thing, so I responded to the next conversation piece. "I'm sorry. I've never heard that word before. Please explain, Miss E.." I implored.

"It means uncontained fervor, enthusiasm, and excitement!" she said with a glow.

"You seem to fit that script."

"It has become a way of life for me. I am Miss E."

"Well, Miss E., Caramel is my real middle name. Most people think it's a nickname," I said.

"Like the candy, honey?" Miss E. burst into a hearty laugh bigger than her frame would allow.

"Well, I never met anyone that sweet before. I'm gonna call you Sugar, Sugar."

"Sugar it is, Miss E. Now what's your story?"

"Why do you think I'm eating this fruit bar, Sugar?" Miss E. asked.

I simply looked at her with questioning eyes. "I really have no idea."

"It's about the simplest thing I've ingested my entire life."

"How so?"

"A fruit bar is exactly what it says it is. I made it myself. I bought some sticks, mashed up some peaches in a blender with a little water and honey, and froze them on the stick inside a mold."

"Sounds healthy," I said.

"Healthy and at face value, unlike adults. The only humans who come to us at face value are children. They are the most innocent when they're born. Then some crazy adult teaches them words and their ideas of morals and values."

"You seem like a very moral person," I suggested.

"Oh, Sugar, I am, but it came with a price. It took me a while to just stick to one book of morals to really understand that I had put too many ingredients in life's fruit bar when all I needed was the simple stuff."

"So that's your story?" I asked.

"That's my story. Keep it simple and you'll have few wrongs to apologize for later."

Her photo shoot was as simple as our conversation. In fact, she went back to her house to bring along two more fruit bars--one for me and another to be featured in her pictures. By the end of her shoot, the frozen dessert was gone and the last shot was of her smiling with her barren popsicle stick. It was just that simple.

By the time Miss E. and I chopped it up, she offered me a chance to come by and visit any time I liked. She revealed to me that she ran away with her younger sister after she got in the *family way* with a child out of wedlock to a black man. She admired her sister's courage and refused to live in a home where babies, no matter how or when they came to the world, were rejected. Miss E. didn't reveal where home was; she just reminded me of the cliché, it truly is where the heart lays its hat.

After telling her what happened to my parents, Miss E. said I could be her surrogate niece because Sarah, Ms. E.'s sister, gave her baby up for adoption.

"It's a shame, really. Sarah and I used to always talk about the life we'd have with our children. They would travel together, attend the best schools, and have the freedom to become whomever they wish. Our parents were socialites and we had to fit into their mold. An interracial baby was not a part of their plan-- especially out of wedlock."

Miss E. zoned out for a moment. I just held her hand and then she cracked a smile.

"Where is your sister now?" I asked.

"Living abroad with my daughter, Rebecca, in some remote Indian village. They are off to Antigua next year," Miss E. giggled.

"What happened to the father of the baby?"

"We're not sure. Rumor has it he died of a broken heart. I think my parents secretly sent him away to keep him quiet."

"By *keep him quiet* do you mean they had him killed?" I said with a gasp.

"Oh, no! My parents were a lot of things, but they were not murderers. They couldn't have blood on their hands."

"What if..." I paused and pulled myself closer to Miss E. "What if your sister and her lover are both living in India?"

"It's possible. Who knows, Sugar? If they are, I hope they are enjoying every bit of their time together and make another baby--at 52. She never did fall in-love with another man or have more children. She, somehow, believed the universe would bring them back together."

"That would make an awesome book and photo collection. Please call me if that happens. I want exclusive shots."

"I will, Sugar. I will."

Back to the Future of 2006

Miss E.'s wisdom and simple way of thinking was exactly why I called her for advice about calling or not calling Jeffrey Banks. His request required a simple yes or no or rather a simple effort on my part to call him. Miss E. made it plain:

"Free food never hurt anyone. Eat, drink, be gone, or if the company is good, go back for seconds," Miss E. said sipping her green tea outside of A Cup O. T Café.

"Miss E., I have enough going on in life. I don't have a steady gig, I have to find some place to live, and..."

"...and what, Sugar? You think life is going to stop because obstacles come your way? Horse shit!"

"Well, uh..." I stumbled upon hearing her curse.

"Sugar, you know as well as I do that all work and no play is a sure sign of complacency. One day, you'll turn around and have all your ducks in a row and you'll be the only one watching them swim in a small body of water that only you can enjoy," Miss E. warned.

"That's not true. You can come over and sit by the lake with me."

Miss E. pursed her lips and looked at me sideways over the rim of her sunglasses.

"I may not have a man, but I go out and enjoy the world. I don't have no time to sit 'round looking at no ducks, Sugar. God won't be catching me at no water. That's for sure. I have to stay busy."

"Miss E., I haven't given my heart to anyone since...well, since my first and last committed relationship."

"Sugar, he asked you out, not to marry him. You and that camera stay so wrapped up in each other, it's no wonder your last name isn't Kodak or something." Miss E. plucked my camera and let out a laugh.

"That's not funny, Miss E." It was. I let out a laugh to myself.

"If you're as sweet as your name, taste a little sugar in your life, and let someone treat you for a moment. If things work out, great. If not, Sugar, go on 'bout your business. Just keep your legs closed until you see his health card, credit score, and you find out he ain't married. Then if you really like him and say *I Do*, call me. That will take 'bout six months. That's how I got my Sammy," Miss E. cautioned.

"You're a trip, Miss E."

CARAMEL'S SUNDAY

"...and a vacation on most Saturdays. Now hand me a few packs of honey so I can take them home. Let's go for a walk before you take me back."

The decision was made. Miss E. made me call Jeffrey before leaving her house. She lay in her burgundy and gold chaise lounge eating a strawberry fruit bar, bobbing her little bare feet and wiggling her pink toes to music she had in her head.

"Hello, Jeffrey. This is Caramel." I decided who I would be.

CARAMEL'S SUNDAY

JPEG 007
One Brick at a Time

Sponsorship Provided by
Tamara Lumpkin
Life Coaching Services
www.tamaralumpkin.com

While Miss E. was convincing, I was not completely ready to date anyone. When I first moved to D.C., I worked as a temp for a marketing company. Once, my supervisor, Tamara Elroy, and I had lunch together. Ms. Elroy was very firm on the clock and quite casual off the clock. Her advice was priceless:

Companionship is like marketing. Promote yourself to the right target audience, and you'll get the desired result.

In essence, while everyone might want the product, you still want to make sure it is in the hands of those who will continue singing its praises long after the hype is over; so take your time with your marketing campaign before you let someone take you off the shelf.

I did just that. Jeffrey Banks appreciated the phone call and completely welcomed the idea of us getting to know each other before breaking bread on a date.

Jeffrey was indeed a busy man. Jeffrey Theodore Banks achieved his life's goals twice, and once more for good measure, by the time he was 38. He was 45 when we met. CPA, M.B.A. and Ph.D. followed his name on three different business cards. In fact, he'd done so well in his lifetime that he only worked six months out of a year and vacationed during the other six. A good year for Jeffrey was spending $300,000 of somebody else's money while making $600,000 he could bank. Rarely did he pay for anything. His pro bono work was not free at all. In lieu of corporate checks from some of the wealthiest, independent companies around the country, Jeffrey accepted full comps at a CEO's condo while he helped him or her maintain good financial standing as the contracted accountant. His net worth was something like $3.5 million after taxes. Now, he just consults on his time. People have to fit into Jeffrey's schedule.

Since his life was so opulent, his decision to take me out gave me pause like a comma after items in a series. He was quite an enigma. I'm sure there were some career gold diggers banging down his door who would willingly give him a moment of pleasure at will.

I was hesitant to disclose too much about myself. What he needed to know, more than anything, was that I still had some living to do. I wasn't ready to settle for anything that would take me away from my American Dream of property ownership, individuality, and my equal share of the financial pie. After putting my cards on the table, Jeffrey assured me that he respected my ambitions.

"I'm not here to take you off course; I just think you would make great company," he said.

"How do you know?" I asked.

"Look how long it took us to have this conversation. Most women would be in my car, home, and pants after our initial contact. Not you. You stood me up when I invited you to meet me in the lobby of the theater," Jeffrey explained.

"I was working," I said while switching lenses on my camera.

"Exactly. I wasn't worth you sacrificing your focus. You didn't need my attention."

"Any self-respecting person would have done the same," I said.

"You'd be surprised. Nothing is sexier than a man with power and money."

"Aren't you confident!"

"So I've been told," he said.

"...and arrogant."

"I've been called worse," Jeffrey said laughing.

"Well, I have goals, and I plan to see them through."

"Good! What can I do to help you get there?" Jeffrey asked.

I was at a loss for words. I wasn't expecting the call to turn into an opportunity to explore career options. I thought he was trying to work his way into my Vickies via a dinner date.

"Well, my Gramps always taught me to shoot for the moon. So, I need a recommendation to secure a business loan for an online art gallery and mobile photography school.

"That's the best you can do?"

"Is that a yes?"

"Call my office in the morning and set up an appointment with my admin assistant. We'll work something out."

"This offer stands without me going out to dinner with you?"

"I've seen your work. The piece that's in Gregorio's home is my favorite. *Heart's Desire?* Yeh, that's it."

Double wow! He had my attention. Because he was bold enough to offer, I was bold enough to call.

The next morning, I called Your Bank, Inc. The administrative assistant penciled me in for a late morning appointment with Jeffrey that day. I was in between jobs and I wasn't scheduled to be in New York for the week, so I made my way to his office in Southeast D.C.

I saved on gas and parking by taking a commuter bus to the Anacostia subway station. Then I took a bus to the office. The bus stop was right in front of 3000 Martin Luther King, Jr. Avenue. He was dead smack in the *hood*.

The community was in full swing. Tardy children in uniforms were rushing to school. Big sisters and brothers had their younger siblings in tow as they crossed the street. Working mothers sprinted to the bus stop in sneakers while making sure they didn't wrinkle their suits before getting to work.

The avenue was not without its local characters-- Begging Bonita or Uncle Charlie. They were high from a recent fix but were harmless. Street law requires you to stay in your lane if you didn't any want trouble. I was glad I left my camera in its bag. I didn't want to appear rude to a neighborhood that looked like it was once developed, but time, politics, and circumstances took over its appearance.

The office building where Your Bank, Inc. was located towered over the vintage brick store fronts with torn signage and barred windows. It was clearly one of the newer constructions on the street. A banner hung above the awning: *Rebuilding the Community One Brick at a Time.*

Upon entering the glass doors, I had the option of taking the stairs or the elevator. I was drawn to the stairs because the walls had framed photographs of the neighborhood. *The Big Chair,* a 19-and-a-half-foot landmark in D.C., was the first photo on the wall. The chair became a symbol for S.E. in D.C. even after the furniture store, for which it was built, closed. I was so caught up with the photos that I hadn't realized I was at the top of the stairs.

Near the glass double doors was a three dimensional model of plans for the neighborhood. There were fiberglass figurines of the people in the community rebuilding the store front businesses and students working alongside residents to plant gardens. There was a blueprint for a movie theater called Eastside Theaters as there were few options for entertainment in Southeast except the local carry-out, sneaker and baby clothes shops, and liquor stores. Because many of the neighborhood recreation centers and playgrounds were either closed or dilapidated, children had no place to play outside of recess; however, the pictures that hung on the brick walls of the building at 3000 Martin Luther King, Jr. Avenue said differently. I was totally and utterly impressed.

"Welcome to Your Bank, Inc., Ms. Moss," Jeffrey's welcome interrupted my thoughts.

"So, *Tommy Ford*, I mean Mr. Banks, this is what you do when you're not running in Hains Point or into my shots?"

"This is only part of what I do. This is the community office. I work with architecture firms that rebuild communities, and community businesses hire me to help them secure grants and funding for renovations," Jeffrey said.

"Please explain," I said.

"In due time, Ms. Moss. First, I need you to sign in with Freda Nu Nu. I'll be ready to meet with you in a moment."

Jeffrey did the ninja move again and was out of sight before I could blink.

Ms. Nu Nu was in position and had me sign in upon my arrival. As aloof as Jeffrey Banks seemed, he was quite the professional. Our phone conversations never disclosed Jeffrey's love for community service.

This actually earned him points. Since being unemployed, I found great value in doing what I love for free at the elementary school in my neighborhood. The owner of my building suggested I volunteer with the Saturday arts program when I first moved to Fort Washington. Because I headed to North Carolina twice a month to serve dinner at the senior center, I built in the time with the kids on alternate Saturdays to help them with painting projects.

Jeffrey walked in right on cue before my mind had another chance to wander. He headed into his office and buzzed the receptionist.

"Mr. Banks is ready for you, Miss Moss," Ms. Nu Nu whispered while bending slightly toward me. Her breath smelled like Christmas--pine and peppermints.

I gathered my things and followed Ms. Nu Nu toward Jeffrey's office.

"Thank you, Ms. Nu Nu," Jeffrey said as she escorted me to a seat.

"My pleasure, Mr. Banks."

I sat quietly waiting for Jeffrey to open with conversation. It was a bit uncomfortable as I was trying to be professional with a man who was at first interested in courting me, or rather, interested in taking me out on a date.

"You were on time," Jeffrey said just after signing a document.

"Did you expect less? I'm timely, Mr. Banks," I said.

"That's good to know. It will make writing the recommendation letter easy."

I cleared my throat hoping I wasn't about to be a part of a scene in a movie where the high-powered business man takes advantage of a young and ambitious woman.

"What do you have in your briefcase?" he asked.

"It's a proposal and business plan," I said with a little hesitation.

Jeffrey let out a laugh. "Relax. I'm not going to bite. Hand over your crafty work. Let's see if you're as great a writer as you are an artist."

I moved quickly and handed him my resume, portfolio of work, and my idea of a business proposal. He remained quiet as he read my documents with a careful eye. He made some marks with a red pen, nodded a few times with a smile, and then closed them up. He sat for a moment, then clasped his hands together. It was a long 20 minutes.

"Well?" I asked anxiously.

"Well..." He bobbed his head in a quick vertical motion.

I leaned in with my eyes. "Mr. Banks, you're scaring me."

"No need. It's not bad. I want to spend a little more time with the proposal, if you don't mind."

"I don't mind. I have a copyright on it."

"Wow! A copyright on a business plan. Talk about C.Y.A.!"

"I'm country, not stupid," I said with a laugh.

"Indeed, Miss Moss. Indeed."

"Can you give me some verbal suggestions while I wait?"

"I sure can..." he said.

"...with no contingencies."

"I wouldn't think of it!" he smirked.

"Good."

"I'd like to see you include headings in your proposal."

"Headings?"

"Yes--to separate your mission statement,

projected start-up investments, the community need for your business--headings."

I took notes as he spoke.

"I know this isn't your final draft, but just make sure you use quality paper. If you use 25% cotton, it will make your presentation look sharper," Jeffrey responded.

"Good point," I said.

"While most banks won't be as concerned about the type of paper you use, they'll notice a difference in yours and someone else vying for the same funds. Stand out in everything you do," Jeffrey continued to share.

"Thanks. That little bit is helpful."

Jeffrey paused for a moment as he searched through his desk. He pulled out an envelope from his drawer.

"Here's an invitation to a black tie I can't attend on Friday. I'll be leaving for Louisiana for a few days. Take my place. You might pick up a few ideas while you're there. Expand your thinking," he suggested.

He was probably going to New Orleans with one of his prospects. I didn't want to engage him too far into his plans because we were still getting to know each other. His kindness left me speechless so I didn't have any words to project from my filled heart.

Jeffrey flashed me a smile and said, "Open it on your way out. I have a meeting in 20 minutes. Call me later so I can RSVP for you."

My mind wandered to blank spaces. There were open doors; I couldn't decide which to walk through. The space in my mind was sound proof. I couldn't hear anything outside the walls that surrounded me. Then a still voice said: *Dreams are built one brick at a time.*

"Ms. Moss? Ms. Moss?" Before me was Ms. Nu Nu snapping me back into reality.

"I'm sorry. I was having a moment," I said.

"No problem. Mr. Banks told me to see to it that you had everything you needed before you left. Is there something I can do for you?"

Something she could do for me? Something she could do for me?

"Yes, ma'am. Actually there is." I slipped the invitation out of the envelope halfway. "Let Mr. Banks know that I can attend the event on Friday.

CARAMEL'S SUNDAY

JPEG 008
Sponsorship Provided By...

I looked at Jeffrey with a different set of eyes. While his ambitions might still include taking me out to dinner, I had another focus. He was a great person to know in business. Daddy's networking genes looked good on me.

The rest of my day was open so I decided to take a trip to see *The Big Chair*. It was located almost 2 miles from Your Bank, Inc., Because the weather was mild, I decided to walk and take in the local flavor.

I had a Digicam and started shooting Anacostia's people, places, and things. There was no need to be formal with the Nikon. The area was truly under reconstruction. The most contemporary building was at the intersection of Martin Luther King, Jr. and Milwaukee Avenues--a charter school. It was located directly across the street from an institution of some kind. Although the buildings were completely gated, several of its residents seemed to dwell on the outside perimeter with their personal belongings near the bus stop.

"Excuse me. What are those buildings called?" I stopped and asked a passerby.

"St. E.'s," the man answered quickly and kept walking.

CARAMEL'S SUNDAY

Before I could ask what the *E* stood for, I saw the sign that read, "St. Elizabeth's Hospital is registered under the National Historic Landmark Program."

The Spanish-tiled roofing on some of the buildings told the story of magnificence some time ago. The boarded windows sealed its history to the public. There was definitely a story behind them. The towers shouted their importance to the cloud. In confinement, those lovely red brick buildings stood elegantly. The grass on the property was thigh high. Even still, its character remained, but it was really in need of some maintenance and life.

Before reaching the site of *The Big Chair,* my stomach urged me to make a pit stop when my nose smelled fresh fish frying. It was coming from a place called Morgan's. The line was out the door. Either Jesus was in there breaking off pieces of fish and bread or it was as good as the yellow marquee suggested:

It's food so great you'll scrape your plate.

"Excuse me," I began to ask the man in front of me sending a text message. He looked at me with sleepy eyes.

"How's the food here?"

"It's straight," he said without lifting his eyes off the QWERTY keyboard.

"Like it's *ah-ight* straight or *slap yo granmama* straight?" I asked in my best urban accent I could muster. I tried to blend in.

"Sweetheart, I wouldn't be standing in this line if it was just *ah-ight.*"

"You have a good point."

"You can't go wrong with the fish sandwich and a side of green beans," he suggested.

"Thanks."

I got a head nod from my neighbor in line and just anticipated my moment at the counter.

While waiting in line, I decided to ear hustle as two women reminisced about the '80s. They had since moved out of D.C. and moved to nearby Prince George's County in Maryland; however, they came to the city once a month to get some good fried fish.

"Girl, the '80s were it!"

"Remember the winter of '86 when we were supposed to march in the MLK parade..."

"...and...and...the blizzard cancelled the plans?"

"Honey, I was ready with my two layers of long Johns, and..."

They spoke in unison, "Electric blue leg warmers."

"Girl, I could hardly get into my majorette boots 'cause my grandma made me put on three pair of tube socks."

"I wonder where Mrs. Cook and Mrs. Epps are these days? They made sure we were in step in every parade."

"I was more excited to see Santa Claus sitting in *The Big Chair*."

"Weren't we all!"

The ladies continued to laugh and chat a bit more before an abrupt reflective pause. The silence was broken and so was my heart.

"Yeah! Too bad Southeast has to live without it for a few more weeks.

I interjected. "I'm sorry. Did you say *The Big Chair* is gone?"

The two women looked at me with side-eyes because it was clear I was listening to their conversation. Busted.

"I'm sorry, ladies. This is my first time in the area and I was really hoping to see *The Big Chair*," I said while trying to redeem myself.

Still not impressed with my cover up, one of the ladies slowly responded, "Yes. *The Big Chair* is gone."

"It is being restored. It's supposed to be rededicated on April 25th," One of the ladies added.

I reached inside my pocket and pulled out a business card in an attempt gain some credibility.

I extended my hand and said, "I'm Caramel Moss, a photographer, and I like to capture the life and people of places I visit."

"Shoot, in that case, I'm a model and need some headshots," the second lady said. She took my card and looked it over.

"The chair is under reconstruction. Some company is making repairs to it so it can last longer. I'm Angie, by the way. I was serious about the headshots. I'm running for Mrs. Maryland," she said.

"Well, be sure to give me a call when you're ready," I said.

"I will," Angie said.

The ladies' voices were a murmur after I was able to get the information I needed. The line moved quickly. There were three people ahead of me, so I decided to completely take the invitation Jeffrey gave me out of the envelope.

The guest speaker was The National Teacher of the Year. The venue was the Grand Hyatt downtown-- the place of a memory from my past. Just before placing the invitation back in the envelope, I noticed familiar words in fine print: Sponsorship provided by Staplers, MSApple, and Brooks Foods. My mind was on pause. Solomon.

"Ma'am! Ma'am!" I heard the faint sound of a person's voice. The cashier was ready to take my order.

"Oh! I'm sorry. I'll have one fish sandwich on wheat, and an iced tea," I said.

She wrote down my order and then asked me for my name.

"Caramel," I told her.

"Ma'am, is your last name Moss?"

"Yes," I replied with a baffled look.

She then handed me a cup of tea and a brown bag.

"Wow! That was fast!" I remarked in shock.

I looked in the bag. Inside was a fish sandwich and a piece of cake.

"You guys give extra service. Was the pie included?" I asked.

"Yes, Ma'am. Your order was called in and paid for."

"Come on lady!" someone shouted behind me.

I put up the *hold-on-one-moment* finger. It was welcomed with a few expletives.

"Who called it in?" I asked.

"Sorry, ma'am. I was sworn to secrecy," she said with a smile. Then she quickly ushered for the next customer. I slowly walked out of the carry-out with a free meal in my hand.

CARAMEL'S SUNDAY

JPEG 009
Zoom! Zoom!

My afternoon moved faster than my zoom lens. One moment I'm meeting with Jeffrey, and then I'm taking his place at a fundraising event where I might see a lost love. Next, I'm in line with a potential client for a photo shoot. The mystery fish is a whole new topic. I'm the queen of donations. Maybe Jesus was inside Morgan's after all.

I had to take a seat in the shade. *The Big Chair* might be gone, but the cement curb outside of Morgan's would have to do for my nerves to calm down.

The odds were great that I'd see Solomon at the fundraiser. More than four years had passed since I sent him the break-up email and photo. In retrospect, it was probably not the most mature gesture. It was, however, the only response I knew he'd hear. Then again, Solomon's hearing was guarded by his ego and his own voice at that time.

"Yeh, baby. I hear you," was a common phrase every time I tried to talk to him about anything important. His inattention to me showed me what was really important to him--handling business on his laptop or Blackberry. It was my hope that we had both grown up a bit if we actually shared the same space again. As much as he didn't want to be like his father, he was turning into him.

My thoughts were interrupted by a car horn. I was so engrossed in my sandwich that it took three more beeps before I looked up long enough to see my cousin Dolly waiting at the traffic light.

"Girl! Get in this car!" she shouted as she began to merge in the lane closer to me.

I scooted off the concrete and rose to meet her. My sandwich was mostly eaten, but I still wrapped the remaining contents to fit in the brown paper bag.

"Where's your car?"

"I took Metro."

"Why are you sitting in the hot sun eating like you're homeless?" Dolly asked.

"I was just getting a little taste of Southeast. The question is, what are you doing on this side of town?" I asked after closing the door.

"Oh, honey, this is about to be the market in a few years. I'm getting my claws in early with these condo conversions and rehab properties." Dolly rolled down the windows of her coupe. She was being polite, but I knew the smell of fish was not her idea of air freshener.

"Where are you headed now?" I flipped through a

few of Dolly's papers. I hadn't the slightest idea what all the real estate codes meant, but I was hoping to see if any of them were commercial properties.

"I'm actually headed your way."

"That makes sense."

"What?"

"The reason you're giving me a ride."

"Mel, even If I weren't headed your way, I'd still snatch your butt off the street. The least I could do is drop you off at a Metro station or take you to your car. That's what I do for family." Dolly twisted her neck and turned to look at me with pursed lips.

"Well, family," I began, "Guess what?"

Dolly struggled to guess after taking a swig of her water.

"You're moving to Africa!" A loud laugh bellowed from Dolly's mouth.

I flicked my fingers to pluck her arm. "No, silly! I got invited to a black tie event on Friday."

"So what's so special about that?" Dolly rolled her eyes.

"Soooo...one of the sponsors is Brooks Foods." I paused to let my words sink in as Klymaxx sang *Meeting in the Ladies Room*.

"Brooks Foods? Brooks Foods?" Dolly's eyebrows were almost shaking hands just before making the connection.

"Oh, my God! Solomon!" Dolly shouted.

"Ding! Ding! Ding! Ding!"

"You haven't seen him since..."

"2000!" We both broke out in a hearty laugh.

"Do you think he'll be there?"

"I don't know, and part of me actually..." I paused and looked out the window to reflect before continuing. Dolly broke the silence as we moved up three car lengths.

"Part of you what, cousin?"

"Part of me misses our friendship."

It was true, and it was at that moment I realized I did miss my friend. The older you get, the more you wonder about the driving forces behind your past self. I broke up with Solomon because...well, because he stopped letting me be myself. It's a good enough reason, but not enough to throw away a friendship that started on the playground of Garysburg Elementary.

"Well, Miss Lady, opportunity seems to be presenting itself for you to either open or close a chapter," Dolly advised before turning up the radio to play Frankie's *Happy Feeling* and letting it blast throughout the car.

I played out two scenarios in my head. My self-righteous mind stood firm and strong and wanted to pretend not to get excited about seeing Solomon. My emotional self jumped for joy to right an immature wrong and reclaim my friendship. My decision to leave that Post-it note-like email seemed justifiable given the circumstances at the time. I didn't want to fit into a mold. I was happy with me. Clothes didn't make me. The core of who I am would remain the same in Gucci, Fucci, or Nada. Whatever the outcome of the possible encounter, I wanted to, at least, walk away in peace. Relationships are truly like roller coasters. The moment you get a grip on the handle bars of it all, the easier the ride. The hills don't seem so steep and scary and you'll put your hands in the air despite the coaster operator's warning, "Keep hands and arms inside at all times."

Just as the music began to fade in Dolly's car, so did I...into a dream where Jeffrey Banks and Solomon Brooks reached through my chest in a race for my heart. Solomon I could understand in the crevices of my mind, but Jeffrey? My subconscious mind had some explaining to do.

CARAMEL'S SUNDAY

JPEG 010
Out of my Shell(y)

"**M**y plane landed early, Mel. So I'll be at your apartment in an hour."

Shelly left a voice mail message for me just 30 minutes before I checked my phone. I had enough time to clean up the guest room before her arrival.

Shelly and I remained friends after college. She decided to take up public relations after receiving a full scholarship from Ball State University in Muncie, Indiana, for her Master's. She liked the Midwest so much she decided to keep moving West and lived in Chicago in hopes of working for Harpo Studios, Inc. After a few gigs at small firms, Shelly decided to take her experience and establish her own company representing local politicians. She was great at what she did, so I hired her to work with me as I figured out the next plans for my work. Her visit was for both business and pleasure. She would get three hots and a cot and a week's worth of entertainment on my dime.

Shelly's visit was also timely because she had an Illinois senator in D.C. who needed her to help him as he developed his campaign for the next presidential election. He was a grassroots politician, and Shelly had both the energy and style to help boost his image beyond the Windy City.

I was going to make the best of the time with Shelly. We'd work hard, then play hard. I definitely had to fit in some time for her to meet Miss E. Shelly's visits, in the past, were fly-by-night. Shelly had visited two other times when she actually stayed over. Otherwise, we'd have enough time to eat lunch on the Hill or at the airport before she departed. I was holding her hostage for girlfriend-time during this visit.

"Open up! It's the PO-LICE," she said in a deep voice while pretending to be law enforcement.

"I know you better stop banging on my door like a crazy woman, Shelly!" I opened the door with a big smile and hugged my hometown homie.

With shades on top of her head, Shelly greeted me with a guilty smile. In tow were her designer bags that needed a room of their own. I'm glad she had a job to support her shopping habit.

"You're only going to be here for a week," I reminded her.

"Maybe...if you're lucky. I've been giving D.C. some serious consideration for relocation," Shelly responded as she made a beeline for her room, as she called it. I followed her while grabbing two of her five bags that were still at the door.

My apartment was large enough for a family of three. So getting to the guest room took a few twists and turns. I made it worth Shelly's time because I left a chocolate mint on her pillow to give the room five-star flavor. She really loved the stuffed panda, a symbol of her sorority, Delta Epsilon.

"You think you know me, huh, Mel?" she joked as she bit down on the mint.

Shelly plopped on the bed as if to make a snow angel.

The bedding in my rooms always made for a nice retreat. In addition to the 800 thread count sheets, I covered the bed with down feather comforters. I'm a stickler for relaxing after a long day. The pillows hug your head when making contact, thanks to memory foam. I bumped Shelly with my hip and joined in the fun.

"So, what's good, Shells?"

"Girl, this and that! I am really just glad to be away for a hot second. Being the mastermind behind the images of so many people can cause a PR professional to start having an identity crisis. I hired an intern to handle things while I'm here."

"You sure that was the right thing to do?" I asked.

"Trust me, I did a thorough check on Gabe before letting him loose on his own. I took him right out of Ball State's alumni base. His professors were my professors. I wanted to make sure that 4.0 wasn't just fluff. I needed someone as thorough as me."

"I see."

"Besides, he has OCD. That means every *i* will be dotted and every *t* will be crossed. You gotta love that about obsessive people."

Shelly didn't like too much attention on herself. This was odd seeing that she always had admirers and people constantly caring about her thoughts. She jumped out of the bed as she began to transition to another topic. She wandered over to an old jewelry box I kept in the guest room. I watched her as she combed through my jewelry, or lack thereof, to see if my style had improved. What she found were the pieces I borrowed and neglected to return to Dolly for Gregorio's premiere.

"I see you keep the same multipurpose earrings in your ear," she snarled as she cut her eyes at me.

"It's real gold, doesn't turn, and gets the job done."

Solomon had bought me a pair of gold hoops for

my high school graduation present. We hadn't started dating yet, so there was no emotion tied to the gift.

"Mm hmm. So the fact that Solomon gave them to you doesn't have aaaaanything to do with you wearing them all the time. Huh?"

"Nope!" I said nonchalantly. I threw one of the pillows at her just before jumping off the bed and heading to my kitchen.

"So, what I want to know is..." Shelly screamed from the guest room.

"Yes, Shelly, I'm still a virgin," I yelled back. That sent her running to where I was. Her running sounded like a small herd of elephants. Ba boom! Ba boom! Ba boom!

I didn't turn to see her expression. I was sure it was a cross between pageant-winner-surprise and shock when realizing you missed your period three weeks after a one night stand.

"Mel!"

"Shelly!"

"I know we're Christians and all, but all these fine, powerful men in the D.C. area and not one of them convinced you out of your drawlz? Mmm...girl, please! I'd give new meaning to Chocolate City and the Underground Railroad!"

"You'd have a serious doctor bill from all the active germs and bacteria jumping in your panties. The ratio of men to women out here is ridiculous. All kinds of cupcakes, pound cakes, and Ho Hos would be falling out your vagina from the yeast infections you'd contract. That's if you're lucky," I said.

"I protect myself, baby girl. Believe that. I hear you, though," Shelly responded in retreat.

"That's not to say I haven't gone out. I even kissed three men since Solomon!"

"WHAT?"

"Don't get excited. They were just pecks. One guy tried to slip me the tongue. It tasted too much like pickles. I had to pass," I said while cringing.

With hands on her hips, Shelly asked, "Pickles, Mel? Really?"

"Really! You know I don't like pickles, relish, nothing with that vinegary taste. I was not turned on."

Shelly washed her hands as soon as she heard the clanking of pans. She knew I was getting ready to make our college classic: fried chicken, homemade biscuits, and fried cabbage. We would pool our money together to get the ingredients once a month rather than indulging in the usual pizza or Chinese campus food. The dessert in the cafeteria was always on point, so we did make it to the cafe before it closed for the night. I let our iced-tea sit over night before adding the sugar. We wanted to taste the tea leaves before we tasted the sugar. We only had to squeeze a little lemon in our glasses to give our tea a twist.

"Move over so I can make these biscuits, sistah! I know what time it is."

It was good having Shelly around. I was equally glad that she'd serve as a great distraction as I prepared for the fundraiser at the Grand Hyatt. Coincidentally, she, too, had an invitation to the affair. While I know she had to do business, it was comforting to know I wouldn't be a lone duck in the water in case I did run into Solomon.

In the middle of me placing the seasoned chicken pieces in the bag of flour and dropping them in the cast iron skillet, my cell rings. J. Banks appeared on the face of the phone.

"I'll get it. My hands are free," Shelly offered.

I was a little hesitant about her knowing about Jeffrey because there wasn't much to tell except that he was good-looking, established, and influential. There would be a million and five questions once I got off the phone with him.

"One moment, please." Shelly passed me the

phone with a cunning smile. Then she whispered, "Oh! We will talk."

"Mr. Banks?"

"Ms. Moss? How'd you like your lunch?"

"That was you? I was wondering who to thank for my free meal ticket."

"Morgan's was my meeting. I'm working with the owner to renovate the spot. It needs a face-lift to keep up with the changes in Anacostia. I saw you from the back and phoned in your order on the ride back to the office."

"How'd you know what I like?" I asked while carefully placing chicken in the skillet.

"I had a hunch, but it sounds like I'm missing a meal now."

"You can hear me cooking?"

"I know the sound of popping grease anywhere. My mama was from Mississippi. She'd deep fry dessert if she could. Why do you think I work out?"

"So you can show off?"

"So you noticed my abs? Not bad for a 45-year-old, huh?"

"I guess," I said without giving into his vanity.

Shelly just continued to eavesdrop during my conversation while preparing the dough for the biscuits.

I gave her the *one-more-minute* finger. She gestured with the *take-your-time* hand. I was her temporary entertainment. I'm sure she was hoping the conversation would lead to me getting laid.

"So I was calling to tell you I'm interested in helping you get your business off the ground. No strings attached. The Anacostia area will be like Georgetown in less than 10 years."

"My cousin was telling me the same thing earlier."

"Who is your cousin?" Jeffrey asked.

"Dolly Hunter. She's a real estate agent."

"Her name rings a bell. Maryland and Uptown sales?"

"Yes. She's adding Anacostia to her listings."

"Smart girl. So anyway, we have to get you going, Violet Caramel Moss."

"Just Caramel."

"Sweet."

"You have no idea, sir."

"Oooh! Are you flirting?" Shelly asked in a whisper, while kneading the dough.

I threw a towel at her.

"Let's do dinner when I get back," Jeffrey

asserted.

"You're just determined to get a dinner out of me. I need you to know I don't drink."

"I don't drive."

"Really, Mr. Banks?" I said in amusement at his counter response.

"Really. I don't. I ride, and I have a driver."

"Well, you can have your driver pick me up next Tuesday..."

"Friday. I'll be gone for a week."

"Sunday, I'm volunteering in North Carolina for the weekend."

"Family birthday party. How about Monday?"

"Monday after next, it is, at 8," I said.

Shelly did the *yes, girl* dance as I confirmed.

"I'll choose the restaurant. Just wear something comfortable."

"Comfort I can do."

"See you then. Ms. Nu Nu will call you next week to get your address."

"Okay. Thanks for calling," I said in a cheery voice.

I tried to hide my enthusiasm. My failed attempt burst into a big grin.

"Oh, my! Did somebody just book a date with a man?"

"Jeffrey Banks sure isn't a woman."

"We have time. The cabbage still has to cook and the biscuits have to go in the oven. I want the background info on this guy."

With a quick spirit and shuffling hands, Shelly was all too happy to get our meal prepared so she could lick her fingers with every juicy detail. I hated to disappoint her. I was still getting to know Jeffrey. I'm sure, with her PR frame of mind Shelly would find some way to embellish the facts to make it all shine.

"Are we doing the country crunchy cabbage in a pan tonight?" Shelly asked.

"If we want to eat soon, it's the only way."

The biscuits are going in the oven, now."

"Honey butter?" I asked.

"You know it!"

My apartment was smelling like a Friday night chicken joint. Because I was only cooking a few pieces, my chicken was nearly done. The cabbage was already cut and frying in the pan with sweet peppers, a little seasoning, and cubed pieces of country ham. Time wouldn't allow us to steam and sit. This country crunchy cabbage idea just developed while we were at

St. Augustine's. It's been our tradition since freshman year. When the meal was finally finished, it was time to eat!

All table manners were out the window as I recapped the story of Jeffrey and me. I described him as an established 45-year-old. Shelly called him a distinguished gentleman. I shared with her his love for rebuilding a low-income area. Shelly preferred to note that he was revitalizing an up-and-coming neighborhood. I blushed when I talked about Jeffrey's incredible physique. Shelly was at a loss for words until she finally decided on calling him my Adonis Hercules who would scoop me in his arms and protect me from harm. For every detail I offered, Shelly gave it an embellishment. I didn't stop her because that was just her nature.

By the end of my brief summary of how we met, Shelly had us off and married at some exclusive resort in a wedding that she planned. Then Solomon, who mysteriously found out about our nuptials, would come in and pledge his undying love for me.

"Girl, my name is not Whitley Gilbert!" I said to her.

"You're right. You are *the* Violet Caramel Moss,

Garysburg's rising star!" She flared her hands toward the ceiling light to illuminate her point.

Shelly Royal is the queen of story creation. You have to love her.

"If you're so middle-of-the-road with Jeffrey, why did you decide to go out with him?"

That was a great question. Why did I decide to go out with Jeffrey? I guess Shelly's energy gave me the courage to jump at an opportunity to do something besides immersing myself in my work. Maybe it was the fact that he cared so much about a community that was not his. Maybe it was his business-savvy ways that made him attractive. Maybe it was the imagery I created when talking about him working out. Maybe I was just trying to grow up.

CARAMEL'S SUNDAY

JPEG 011
The Fundraiser

Sponsorship Provided by
L. Katrina Jewelry
www.lkatrinajewelry.carbonmade.com

Messing around with Shelly, I was able to come up with a name for my company, E.Y.E. Studios, Everything You Envision. Shelly helped me design a logo for my business cards and stationary. She also reached out to her network of human resources to find an affordable web master. Within five hours of conducting the search for my web designer, I had a front and contact page. The rest of the site would remain under construction until I finished writing my mission statement. All of this cost me no less than $1,500 and a promise to go shopping for a new wardrobe to brand both my personal and professional images.

"Just because you like the relaxed look doesn't mean you lose style," Shelly argued.

I don't disagree with her assertion, but I just don't believe in paying more than necessary for things I'd outgrow. I am perfectly fine mixing and matching quality pieces that I already own. Shelly helped me see that if I am to be successful, I had better get used to being in pictures as well as taking them.

"It's never a good look to get caught in the same look in multiple places. Change it up, honey. Keep them guessing what's in your closet. Go glam as a creative artist. If nothing else, you'll change people's view of artists and photographers," Shelly insisted.

Her real motive was to prepare me with something to bring to the table when I met with Jeffrey on a more formal level. The more professional I looked, the more serious I appeared in the eyes of investors.

Because I am allergic to confrontation, Shelly and I reached a compromise. I would go shopping, but I did not want to spend any more than $1,000 on my new wardrobe. Part of that budget included my formal for the fundraiser because I still had to get my hair done, and I would splurge on a simple manicure and pedicure. The total fundraiser budget was set at $375. We saved money because the second dress I bought in 2000 with Solomon's money was still hanging in the closet; it was timeless. She agreed to the deal, and when it was all said and done, I had $150 left to spare.

**

Miss E. once told me to always stay in my lane like a race horse. Maintaining tunnel vision is one way to assure that I'd move toward the direction of the finish line. I had to keep this in mind as I made my entrance into the Grand Hyatt's ballroom on the evening of the fundraiser. When the doors opened to the Independence

Hall level of the hotel, everything about the scene was busy.

Clanking glasses of champagne sang in concert with the sips from the lips of guests in intimate circles. Waiters dressed in their penguin suits and white gloves who used nonverbal cues to acquire the attention of anyone who wanted a napkin-full of the hors d'oeuvres. I like to call them mini meats and tiny breads. In the mix of the hustle, or rather at the end of my tunnel leading to the ballroom was an unexpected sight. Jeffrey Banks stood with a relaxed demeanor leaning into the ear of a model-like figure who stood eye-to-eye with him. They both shared glowing smiles when he backed away from her ear and ushered her to extend her hand to some mover-and-shaker in the room.

Jeffrey was supposed to be out of town on business. It was, after all, the reason he couldn't make it to the shindig. His attendance shouldn't have mattered to me; yet, it did. I couldn't help but wonder what kind of show he had been producing with me as the side chick in a supporting role. He had made a few attempts to go out with me, so I didn't know what to make of his appearance with this beautiful statue standing next to him. *Tunnel vision.* I had to keep my focus. I was there to network and learn.

I continued to make my way to the registration area so that I could get to my table. The three-inch Louboutins I borrowed from Shelly were more comfortable than I imagined. I remembered the catwalk moves I learned in Suber Hall at St. Augustine's some years back. My steps were calculated and smooth. The black platforms complemented my black evening gown trimmed with gold butterflies and accent jewelry by L. Katrina. Cita, one of Dolly's best friends, styled my hair in a rain forest of curls pinned with a simple butterfly clip on both sides of my head.

"Caramel Moss," I said to the attendee at the registration desk while fluttering my eyes.

"Yes, ma'am. You're at table two."

Wow! I peered into the ballroom and saw that I was sitting pretty close to the podium. I was glad, for once, that I stepped things up a notch on my attire. I was sure to be in pictures with the media present. My confidence level rose. I was equally glad I was on my A-game because Jeffrey had a plus-one on his arm. Again, I shouldn't have cared, but I sort of did.

I imagined what I would say to him without being obvious about my new found emotion--slightly green-eyed. Did I extend my hand with professional politeness or did I reach out with one of those *shi shi foo foo* hugs and kiss on both cheeks? I wasn't quite sure. So I just did what I usually did in those situations; I did what was natural. I waited for him to approach me.

I felt a gust of wind from a few turning heads as I made a bee-line for my seat up front. A few whispers and side-eyes were made as my slightly thigh-high split opened and closed as I walked. I was almost sure one of the whispers came from Jeffrey because I heard a quick,

"Excuse me for a moment; I see someone I know," pass through my ears. A slight tap on my shoulder quickly followed. I swung my curls slowly as I prepared my smile.

"Hello, Mel Caramel! It's been a long time."

There was only one person in the entire world who called me that name. It was the voice of security when a girl fell in the sand and scraped her knee. It was the voice of a crossroad. I turned to present myself to my past.

"Solomon Montgomery Brooks."

CARAMEL'S SUNDAY

JPEG 012
The Other Banks

I was so focused on Jeffrey noticing me that I completely forgot Brooks Foods was one of the official sponsors of the fundraiser. It was inevitable that someone from corporate would be in attendance. If corporate came, there was also a great chance Solomon would show up to support his family. His eyes interlocking with mine confirmed my predictions.

In the six years since our last meeting, he cut off his hair, except his beard. Looking like Common, his GQ-front-page image totally went *Fortune* meets *Vibe*. The essence of his Polo cologne sent me riding into a memory of happiness. It was like seeing him for the first time on the playground when I was eight and he was ten years old. I had sand in my hair from falling off the swing and into the sand box. He smiled to help me up and asked, "Are you okay?" Even more shy and reserved then, I just nodded, looking up at him with eyes welling with tiny tears of embarrassment.

Now, here I was, years later, looking like the antithesis of how I usually present myself--*funky fresh dressed to impressed ready to party*. I'm sure I caught Solomon by surprise. Like Darrell Cador's book; The seasons changed in both our lives.

"Look at you!" Solomon sang with a smile.

"Look at yourself, sir."

We spoke as old friends as if our break-up never happened. I was surprised he didn't have any choice words for me. He was right to have said a few; he was, at least, at liberty to question my exit from the same hotel where we currently stood.

"Did I pay for that dress?" he asked.

I grinned shyly and said, "Yes, Solomon. I'm afraid you did."

Changing the subject, I asked, "What are doing here? I thought you were still in New York."

"I am," he said nonchalantly.

"I guess you're here to support the family business," I probed.

"That and I'm managing Tonya Banks's modeling career. She's hosting tonight."

I softly gulped as he pointed in the direction of Jeffrey and his *date* with the stunning red spaghetti-strapped dress. At least I was right about her being a model, but what was her connection to Jeffrey given they shared the same last name? Sister? Niece? Daughter? Wife? She was certainly young enough to be a sister, niece, or daughter and just above legal age to be married to Jeffrey. If he was married, I am glad I didn't invest too much stock in his words. I'm a lot of things, but a home-wrecker, I am not.

Tunnel vision. "Is Tonya any relation to Tyra?" I asked with a firm focus.

"No. We checked, but we're still running with the last name. Marketing is easy when you have a name you can cash. No pun intended," Solomon said.

"You can take that to the bank!" I laughed with a snort of sorts. Solomon placed his hand on my shoulder in support.

"You know you're still corny, right?" he asked.

"I'm hilarious!"

"Let's catch up later. I'm in town until next Tuesday. The number hasn't changed." Solomon winked and hurried off in the direction of the Banks family.

He was right. I knew the number by heart. Solomon's mobile phone number had not changed since we were in high school. That thing was the size of a microwave, but he had a cell phone when most of us couldn't afford a beeper.

If the saying *time heals wounds* is really true, Solomon exemplified forgiveness in a way I couldn't have imagined. I was so impressed with the way he handled our first encounter since the break-up. I realized, just in that moment we shared, how immature my exit from the relationship was after seeing his smile and rejuvenated spirit. He had truly moved on with no questions asked.

Before I had any more time to reflect, I got a surprise grab to my waist!

"I sure hope you'll save me a dance, hot stuff!" Shelly plays too much!

"Girl, I 'bout had a heart attack!" I jumped and jolted at her touch.

"Listen to you, returning the Carolina twang to your tongue."

"Unlike some folks, my roots aren't buried deep. Yours took the underground railroad in route to Chicago," I said.

"Now, Caramel, you know I couldn't pass as a city slicker with my country accent," Shelly said in defense.

"I'm still working to keep my southern flavor in Chocolate City too, honey. It was hard to do when I was in New York with..." I paused because a quick memory trailer was cueing up in my mind.

"Oh! Sweety! I saw that fine thing just talking to

you. That's why I had to come over and distract you for a minute." Shelly rubbed my exposed back in comfort.

"Yeh. I guess." I started picking at my French manicure long enough to chip the white tip off my thumb nail. I hid my hand behind my back like a child who was caught before Shelly noticed.

Shelly gently snatched my arm back in front to refresh the paint with her emergency polish she just happened to have in her clutch.

"You are my greatest masterpiece, honey. This is quick dry polish. Now, twirl for Mama, baby!"

Shelly took my hand, and spun me around like a ballerina inside of one of those dainty pink jewelry boxes. I sure felt like a star dancer.

"I am pretty hot!" I joked.

"You are wearing those CLs, sister! Don't get too comfortable. I will need those back before I return to Chicago."

"Have you seen my new and improved walk?" I sashayed for Shelly so she could see the fruit of her labor since her stiletto tutelage at St. Augustine's. I will admit that I practiced a bit before the fundraiser. I impressed myself. Stepping out of the box didn't feel as uncomfortable as I had imagined. I was a willing participant. Maybe that made the difference.

The lights flickered in the ballroom to signal the beginning of the program. Shelly kissed me on the cheek and headed for table 10. We could see each other, but we could not exchange words without proper decorum. I took my seat at table two in front of the table tent displaying my name and title--*Caramel Moss, CEO of E.Y.E.*

As I slid into my satin-covered seat comfortably, there was a little extra pressure added to the back of the chair from a pair of strong hands. They belonged to the same person with a smile I captured at the premiere of *Capitol Offense*--Jeffrey Banks.

"Hello, there, Ms. Moss!"

"Evening, Mr. Banks." I remained fully composed as I looked from him to the stage to see Tonya Banks.

"You look amazing," he whispered as he took his seat.

"I know," I whispered back without flinching.

He was caught off-guard, but still maintained a smile.

"You must be a teleportation specialist," I said with an inquisitive tone.

"What makes you say that?" Jeffrey asked.

"You are supposed to be in Louisiana."

"I changed my mind, and I'm glad I did." His eyes

of seduction clued me into the reason why he was glad.

"I bet."

"Do you know Tonya Banks, tonight's emcee?" he asked.

"Your wife?"

"My niece. I've never been married unless you count that one time in junior high school when we pretended to care for a family with an egg as a child."

"Very funny," I responded.

"No. What's funny is you thinking Tonya was my wife as if you cared."

I put my index finger up to my lips to let him know I was giving my full attention to the stage. It was also my way of avoiding his comment. Maybe I cared a tad, but that was not for him to know. That was for me to process and decide if I really cared or was just curious.

Niece Tonya was even more beautiful and elegant now that I knew her full identity. She welcomed us with a centerfold smile and cosmetically perfect voice. Protocol dictated that she thank all the sponsors responsible for financing the event and ticket holders who made an investment in the Art for Hearts Project (AHP) through the Langston Neale Foundation.

CARAMEL'S SUNDAY

The evening included exhibitions of both visual and performing arts by the students from 12 area middle and high schools in D.C., Maryland, and Virginia. Their goal for the project was to bring awareness about early detection of heart and kidney disease through diet and exercise. It was a bold and ambitious cause, but with the Department of Health and Human Services and the Commission for Arts and Sciences fully supporting the cause, the project was able to raise more than $3 million in matching funds from outside sources. $100,000 of that donation came from none other than Jeffrey Banks.

My ticket was worth $5,000. The menu had top-of-the-line fare: Vietnamese prawns and hearts of palm salad, bacon-wrapped filet mignon, pan-seared salmon with lemon-mint dressing, rice pilaf, grilled vegetables sautéed in garlic butter, warm rolls with honey butter, and my bottomless unsweetened iced tea. Judging by the placement of Jeffrey's hand on my thigh, my free ticket was going to cost me a little more than the meal.

I leaned over and whispered in his ear, "I'm still a virgin, sir."

I helped Jeffrey remove his hand; he sat up straight and adjusted his tie. He locked at me with cunning eyes and whispered back, "In that case, love, your stock just went up. I'll wait."

CARAMEL'S SUNDAY

SLEEP STAGE 3

Deep sleep. Building up physical and mental energy. This is where the body gets rest.

-The Center for Sound Sleep

CARAMEL'S SUNDAY

JPEG 013
Playgrounds, Business Deals, and Love:
The Solomon Montgomery Brooks Side of the Lens

**Sponsorship Provided by
DDS Holdings**
http://www2.5linx.net/AskDDS/

I always knew Caramel was a bit unorthodox in her methods. She was never one to follow the crowd, but pulling a *Sex in the City*-like move with a break-up email was unexpected. I was completely caught off-guard seeing the engagement ring sitting on the king-sized bed in my hotel suite. There it sat, the marquise cut amethyst, haunting me with memories of the day she asked me to leave the diamonds for those who needed to feel *that* important. She just wanted something spiritually beautiful to shine as a symbol of our connection. With the ring off her finger, she and I were disconnected.

I remember the first time I met Caramel. I forced my dad to let me to tag along with him to oversee a food delivery at Garysburg Elementary School in North Carolina. I was in a suit and tie that mirrored Dad's. I wanted out of it so badly. Because Dad was such a professional, I knew he'd get agitated at my fidgeting and struggles to loosen the tie. At 10 years old, I was pretty sharp and knew Dad would spend at least a half-an-hour or more with the food manager. Numbers could not be rushed when it came to inventory. Dad hated whining, but my silent pant-shake prompted him to shoo me away to the playground nearby. That's when I saw her.

I ran over to the sliding board to climb for a better view. Just before my suede loafers hit the metal ladder, I heard a thump and sliding sound where the pretty girl in yellow coveralls was just swinging into the sun. She fell into the sandbox. Her eyes, big and brown, looked in my direction. I hurried to her without hesitation.

"Are you okay?" I asked. It was a dumb question because the tears were beginning to stream down her face.

"Yeh, but I think I broke my body," she said.

There were no visible signs of broken limbs. I'm sure her body was in shock from the fall. The tears were probably triggered by the specks of sand that got in her eyes from the slide and splash into the sandbox.

"I think you'll be okay," I said to assure her.

"No, I won't! Look at my knee. It's broken."

Her smooth caramel skin now bared a scar in the shape of a heart. It was adorable. I wanted to color inside the shape of the scar to give her back her skin.

"Here," I began, as I extended my hand. "Let me help you."

"I'm scared. What if I can't walk anymore?"

"You will." Our eyes locked as I kept holding out

my hand. After a brief silence, she put her hand in mine, and I helped her regain balance.

"See there...you'll be as good as new. Say, what's your name anyway?"

Sniff. Sniff. She wiped her nose on her sleeve. I knew then she was no typical girl. That was a dude move right there. I gave her my handkerchief that was tucked inside of my jacket pocket. She blew her nose as if we were old friends.

"What's yours first?" she asked lifting her eyes to meet mine again.

"Solomon," I said.

"Mel. Caramel."

"Your whole name is Mel Caramel? For real?" I asked with bucked eyes after jumping back and forgetting that she was using my body for balance. Mel Caramel almost fell again before I quickly caught her.

"No. My whole name is Violet Caramel Moss. People call me *Mel* for short."

"Moss like floss?"

"What's floss?" she asked with inquisitive eyes.

"It's a dental tool to get the ucky stuff out your teeth."

"Oh! Tooth string?"

I giggled. "Yeh! Tooth string."

"I guess, then."

I helped her to one of the benches near the swing so she could rest her knee. We talked about our favorite cartoons and why He Man or She-Ra could beat each other up. It was clear that Mel Caramel thought a woman could do anything a man could do because God gave women extra powers over men.

"Men are supposed to protect women. That's why we have all the muscles," I contested.

"Oh, yeah? Well, women can have babies and that makes them stronger. My aunt had two babies to come out of her on the same day. I never saw a man do that."

She had a point. I didn't have anything to retort her comment so I just resumed to inquiring more about her name after engaging in a stare contest. She won.

"So where did the name Caramel come from?" I asked.

"My auntie told me that my mom ate it a lot when she was pregnant with me, but I never saw her eat it."

"That's strange."

"I said the same thing."

"I thought it was because your skin is like a Sugar Daddy candy stick."

"Is that made out of caramel?" she asked.

"I think so."

"Cool. I didn't know that. I'm not allowed to eat candy," she said shyly.

"Can I call you Mel Caramel anyway? I think it's pretty cool."

She stared at me, then at the clouds, then at me again, and said, "Yeh. I guess it's okay since I probably won't see you again."

"You don't know that." I said,

"Nuh unh! You're not from here."

"I sort of am. Kinda."

"No, ya ain't!" Mel Caramel shook her head in disagreement.

"How you figure?" I asked.

"'For one, it's my first time seeing you. For seconds, you don't come to the town cookouts. And for thirds, I've never seen you at school. People who live around here go to the same schools.'

"Okay, I don't live around here, but I come around here with my dad. So you might see me."

"MMM hmmm," Mel Caramel said, while looking to the clouds again.

Time seemed shorter than I calculated. Just as I was getting to know more about Mel Caramel or Violet

Caramel Moss, Dad signaled me with his Woody Wood Pecker whistle.

"I have to go, but do you play here all the time?"

"Only on Mondays."

"What about Tuesday through Sunday?"

"It depends on who's outside to play with. I am out here waiting on the train on Mondays."

"Why?"

She answered me with silence and continued looking at the clouds. I didn't pry. I didn't understand, but I left it alone.

"Well, maybe I'll see you again. I hope you feel better."

"Thank you for helping me."

I ran back to my father while looking back at Mel Caramel and almost crashed into the delivery truck. If Dad had not shouted, "Solomon! Look out!" I would have had a shiner for sure.

"Son! I need you by my side so you can one day run Brooks Foods..." his voice trailed off in the car as we drove away. I kept watch out the window as I saw Mel Caramel limp her way toward the train tracks. It was 3 o'clock. I wish I could have held her hand to safety. There was nothing I could do to get to her hand again until I set a plan in motion for my future with her.

First, as her best friend, but later as the woman I would ultimately marry. It was love at first sight.

Brooks Foods, Incorporated, housed satellite business offices in Garysburg, North Carolina. It was the low property taxes that attracted my great-grandpa, Vincent Wellington Brooks. He was a Richmond man, but he traded in his roots to make sure he had the best return on his investments. Moving to Garysburg also made sense because my dad wanted to expand his business ventures beyond food and enter commercial real estate.

"Overhead will kill a business, Solly. Always remember that your business can't take care of business if you're always paying high rent," Grandpa Vince would remind me.

We lived in Emporia, Virginia; Dad was one of seven Brooks men who ran Brooks Food, Inc. He was the regional director for the Southeastern region and point of contact for the buyers in Virginia and North Carolina. The home-base for his region was Garysburg, North Carolina. Dad commuted back and forth from Emporia because Mom didn't want him to be so close to work that he'd forget to come home. Since I knew Mel Caramel and I would have no chance of seeing each other on days she didn t commit to the swing, I made it my business to see that dad was prompt for his monthly visits to Garysburg Elementary School.

I'd rush home from school to put on my suit and tie, have dad's briefcase prepared and ready to go. Dad threw his keys in the driver's seat so he didn't have to worry about wasting time looking for them.

"You sure are an eager beaver these days, son."

"I just want to make sure I don't miss out on any opportunities to learn, Dad."

"Are you sure this has nothing to do with that young lady you helped last month, son?"

I was dumbfounded. I hated lying to my father. He could see clear through my thoughts, so I openly admitted that Mel Caramel was my driving force behind my zeal to get to Garysburg.

With embarrassed eyes, I confirmed Dad's suspicion.

"Sir, it has everything to do with her. I think she's pretty. Even with those overalls on...Dad, I think I'm in-love."

"Son, love and business should be kept separate. I will, however, let you in on a little secret."

Dad revved the engine, pulled out of the garage, and had me waiting for the secret until we hit the main street.

"Dad!" I elevated my voice with anticipation.

He giggled. "Oh! Yeh. The secret."

"Yeh, Dad! What is the secret?"

"Your mom and I decided to move to Garysburg at the beginning of the school year."

"You mean...?"

"I mean, you'll be helping me run the business a little more because your new school and the office are close by. You'll have plenty of time to play on the playground AFTER our work is done."

"Will I be going to Garysburg Middle for sixth grade?"

"Son, of course not. You will attend Harrington Halifax Preparatory Middle School until we find an adequate high school. You're a Brooks. We always attend private institutions of learning; it's tradition."

It was in that moment that I decided I'd follow tradition until high school. I knew I would be old and bold enough then to plead my case for attending a public school. I had to make a plan to break the mold of a Brooks man by using my father's words against him. "The bottom line is what matters, son. Always find a way to save money without lacking quality."

Between homework, golf and lacrosse lessons, piano practice, foreign language tutorials, and helping dad run the business, I had little time to rest. Yet, I didn't care if I had only two minutes of sleep if it meant I could play with Mel Caramel. I just wanted to be in her presence. She held secrets I wanted to know unlike the other girls in my elite circle whose economic pedigree seemed more important to those in my world than what was on their heart. The governor's daughter and the senator's niece were beautiful, but just too perfect, like a nun's attendance at church. Yet, Mel Caramel was a circle and a square wrapped into one--she had round edges but came with a straightforward attitude. Even with that, she had feelings.

Her male cousins welcomed me on the field and court to play with them when they realized rich boys had game too. They became more like brothers. They really loved me when I was able to invite one friend to the academy dances. I had to take turns on picking cousins throughout the year because Mel Caramel had a lot of male cousins. Because they were cool with me, they let me be cool with Mel Caramel as long as I didn't cross any inappropriate lines. I knew their loyalty would always be with blood.

Mel Caramel had an armored exterior, but something happened to get her there. I was certain that, beneath it all, she was a vulnerable kitten stuck in a tree. I just had to allow her to fall to safety without having to expose or chip her claws. My dad had designed my perfect mate for me, in his mind. My mom wanted me to be happy. Even at age 10, I knew what I wanted. How is that possible? You just know when you know.

I was able to convince Dad to give me one hour of play time each week when we moved. I spent 30 minutes with Mel Caramel and 30 minutes with her cousin. If I were able to follow him on his runs and give an accurate account of our business matters with Brooks Food, Inc., I could enjoy my end of the bargain.

My job was to calculate the estimated gains and losses with each buyer in the state of Virginia. The Garysburg cluster schools were our last accounts to handle at the end of the month. I had my estimated projections completed a week before our visits with the schools. I was on Dad's schedule so I could report the numbers to him and make updates he deemed necessary. This was our song and dance for three years. By my 13th birthday, I was sitting in the board meetings offering suggestions, flying with him to meet the other Brooks brothers at quarterly retreats to discuss the future of the company, along with their sons and, in a rare case, a daughter, and I was still able to work up a plan to get closer to Mel Caramel.

I made my move when I knew I would have his undivided attention. Dinner time was best. It was just after the Weekly Business Journal segment on the news when I petitioned for my chance to choose.

"Dad, I'll be 14 soon, and I think it's time I start making plans for my future."

Mom looked at me with detective eyes. My sister, Angela, was too young to understand what was about to happen. At four years old, blowing bubbles in her glass of milk was all the excitement she needed.

"Son?"

"I want to go to public school next year."
Dad was composed. He took a swig of his wine, looked at my mom. She shrugged her shoulders because she had no clue where I was going with my gesture to go above the law. So I continued.

"I'm planning to attend Dukem, on scholarship."

"Scholarship? Son, we have plenty of money to pay for your education. What has gotten into you?"

"Dad, I am well aware of the financial security of this family. I will not feel complete if I lean on that security as I come into my manhood. I want to stand on my own two feet, or at least give myself a chance to try."

There was deafening silence. Even Angela stopped blowing her bubbles. Either she had just arrived at some infinite wisdom from my comment or the bubbles were no longer fun.

"Solomon," Mom began. "What is your plan?"

Mom was right on cue with her question. Dad just wiped his hands on the white linen table cloth bearing the gold-embroidered family crest. I reached in my lap for my portfolios and presented them to my parents. I laid out a 10-year prospectus that detailed my education from high school through college and my first years out of Dukem.

"Going to a public school makes me eligible for public funding as well as the Green House Impact scholarship with estimated scholarship earnings of $50,000 a year. Ryland L. Greene is one of the top business men in media and offers this scholarship to students attending public high schools who want to matriculate at private institutions like Dukem University," I advocated.

"Media? Son we're in the business of food."

"Well, about that dad..."

Dad vigorously moved his chair back, slammed his fist on the table, and demanded, "Enough, Solomon."

He scared Angela. A bubble splashed up her nose. Mom's wine spilled over. I stayed composed. Any sign of weakness would reveal my spirit. I was crushed I couldn't finish discussing my plan, but I was not going to give in.

"Dad!" I arose from my seat. "You are the one who taught me that we are more than food. You were the one who said it must have been destiny that you were not named after Great-Grandpa because you're slightly different from your brothers. You were the one who added real estate to the family business. You are the one who is always telling me to think bigger and better. That's what I'm doing. Using my resources to expand on the name so we aren't one-dimensional. The country is changing. Two things our world will need is food and entertainment, even when the economy tanks."

Dad turned to face me. He straightened the bottom of his white-collared shirt and said, "Son. I need a minute."

I looked at Mom. She looked at me. We both looked at Dad walking away. Mom saw the conviction in my eyes and connected with my energy. Angela was confused but simply went back to her bubbles.

"I'll talk to him." Mom ushered Angela to get Miss Dina, our housekeeper, to clean up the table.

CARAMEL'S SUNDAY

Dad eventually saw things my way once he saw the scholarship opportunities were more plentiful if I attended a public school. We agreed that I would not apply for anything that would limit the chances of a student who did not have our financial advantages. In the event I was in competition with someone at my school who applied but was rejected for the scholarships, Dad would cut a check from my trust fund and give it to that student as an anonymous donation.

There was an unspoken plan not mentioned in my plan. I wanted to be closer to Mel Caramel. I would have a two-year start over her. Her high school transition would be smoother with me as her best friend. I would have control over how I wanted my story to begin and end with her. That was the part I didn't work out-- controlling our story. A wise person once said the moment you think you have everything under control is the moment you lose control.

After years of friendship our fellowship turned into a romantic relationship during our college days. I might have gotten comfortable and forgot my Mel Caramel was rather stuck in her ways and could never be forced to conform.

CARAMEL'S SUNDAY

Our friendship was founded on basic values--trust and open communication. Our relationship did not lack love, it just wasn't the affectionate passion you see on television. While I was an extrovert, Mel Caramel was definitely an introvert. It took her more time to process information before making decisions. There were times, however, when I'd push the envelope too far, and Mel would quickly remind me to back off with a quick, sharp glance or a firm, "Solomon, you're crossing a line." There was no indication from her on that fall afternoon that I had traveled off base. I simply asked her to change clothes to look more presentable while we socialized during Howard University's homecoming events. I offered to pay for her expenses; she smiled and took the money I gave her to go shopping.

It only took me six months from the time she broke up with me to realize I had made comments about her casual look too often that might have made her feel like I didn't accept her individuality. In the same breath, I was just trying to encourage her to wear clothes that not only commanded authority but also turned heads. I wanted her to be my wardrobe equal. Mel was consistent with her denim and t-shirt look with a bouncy, wavy ponytail. The denim would come in the form of a jump suit--skirt, or a pair of jeans. She would mix things up every once in a while with a pair of black slacks, dress shirts, and flats. The ponytail would then be transformed into long, wavy, red tresses that hung below her shoulders. She rarely deviated from her look. Mel was not into fashion. She was who she was. Take her or leave her alone.

Her actions spoke louder than words on the day she left our friendship and relationship on my hotel bed. I mulled over whether or not to chase her or let her go. I chose to wait on her to change her mind. The evening into a day. A day turned into a week. A week turned into months. A year to the date of her leaving, I had to devise a new plan to get her back. All of my moves would be calculated and every player in my attempt to get Mel back would be intentionally targeted. In the meantime, I still had to make my money and build a successful career I could be proud to announce to the world. I also had to prove to my father that the entertainment industry was just as sustainable as the food industry.

"Shelly?"

"Yes? Who's this?"

"Solomon Brooks."

"Sol! It's three in the morning."

"I know. I need to find Mel."

"Oh, yeh! About that..."

"Yeh. About that..."

"Call me later in the day. We'll talk."

That next morning came and went to several tomorrows passed. I couldn't bring myself to ask Mel's best friend to be a messenger for me. I remember my mom sharing a cautionary statement, "If you ever want to make God laugh, make plans." While my plan, all those years ago, to get closer to my Mel Caramel was successful, sustaining the relationship failed. So, I decided to take head to Mother's advice and pray.

CARAMEL'S SUNDAY

JPEG 014
Lighting Change

CARAMEL'S SUNDAY

I was willing to risk a limb to go out on a limb to rekindle a flame that once was lit for me. The Grand Hyatt was the perfect background for a new episode. I learned in a film class that every movie has a scene that appears twice. The woman I let get away sat just a few tables away in the same hotel where she left me.

My client, Tonya Banks, was comfortable on the stage sitting pretty as the Mistress of Ceremonies listening to the Teacher of the Year speak. For a moment, I daydreamed about what life would have been like with the former love of my life. I rarely saw her dressed in formal attire. This time I paid close attention to every inch of her, even the slow motion in which she whispered into the ear of Jeffrey Banks, a major contributor to Tonya's career--her uncle. If I didn't know any better, Jeffrey and I were looking out of the same pair of lenses. They were caramel-colored glasses.

His hand slowly moved up her thigh. A little envy tugged at my heart; I thought to jump up to address the matter, but Mel was the same as ever--no nonsense. Her reflex was still good. His rejected hand was quickly returned to its original stance--in his own lap. Then he smiled and whispered back to her.

She mouthed, "I'm not that girl..." I imagined she added a "sir" at the end of the corrective statement. That was my Mel, polite with firmness and a sweet southern eye. She wasn't argumentative, but you knew she meant business. I later learned that a quite agreeable Caramel was the most dangerous Caramel--sweet and sassy.

Accompanied by a smirk, her silence was deadly.

I sat through the pomp and circumstance of the fundraiser that my family's money co-sponsored. I'd get Caramel's story later, but in the meantime, I was patient to wait until the deejay took over and invited attendees to the dance floor. During our time apart, I learned a few moves that would render any woman weak.

After the formalities of the fundraiser, I shadowed Tonya as she worked the room. I carried the business cards; she flashed the smiles for social photographs to be placed on her Myspace web page. Tonya covered a lot of ground in 20 minutes. It helped that she spoke as well as she looked. As I steered her toward the bar to get a drink, the deejay announced he was going on break, but the Platinum Band would keep the party going.

The dancers, full of wine and top-shelf liquor, jammed to the beat of the percussions, the harmony of the keys on the keyboard, and the perfect vibrating sounds from the guitar strings. The lead female vocalist shouted, "It's Electric!" The band kicked things off with the ever-popular Electric Slide. Line dances always drew people to the floor.

It was fun watching the older dancers patiently struggle to learn the steps. The Cha-Cha Slide was next on their playlist. It was a favorite from one lady who shouted, "Chi-Town!" and took off her shoes and nearly broke her ankle trying to keep up with steps. A man just grabbed her and kindly returned her to her seat.

To keep the party going, the band's lead male vocalist stepped up to the mic, greeted and thanked everyone for their contributions for the evening's event. Then the excitement could not be contained when he sang, "You make me happy..." It was all the audience needed to hear before the tables cleared and the bar emptied. Frankie Beverly and Maze's *Before I Let Go* moved the crowd faster than Erik B. and Rakim. Even though the song was older than Tonya, she left me standing at the bar with her drink and the tab.

"You got this, right, Solomon?" she asked rhetorically. She didn't stand around long enough for an answer. I just paid the bartender, sipped on my rum and Coke with one elbow on the counter, and swiveled my drink around as I people-watched.

"She your girlfriend?" the bartender asked.

"Nah, man. Client," I said and sipped without looking up.

"You hit that? You look like a playa, playa!" he said, followed by a screeching laugh as if we were boys.

I forced myself to look up from my glass because I didn't get a good look at the bartender the first time I ordered my drink. I knew I was talking to a dude, but his comment showed his age. I knew he was an amateur trying too hard.

He looked fresh out of college.

"What you know about hittin' and not hittin', bruh? You just turned, what? 21 two days ago?" I asked while laughing and sipping.

"Actually, I'm 25."

"Alright! Did you finish school?"

"I started at Howard, but I didn't finish." He seemed embarrassed so I let up.

"You should make the sacrifice so you can own a bar and not just work at one."

"You sound like my pops!"

"The way I see it, you have a father in your life who cares. You should listen to him. Just get me another rum and Coke. On the rocks! You don't need to know my business." I finished up the last swig before handing him my glass.

I felt compelled to school the young brother on his language in the presence of guests next. Before I could open my mouth again, he beat me to the punch.

"Wait a minute. You're S. Brooks, the entertainment guru from New York City!"

He flung his towel to hang over his shoulder with his left hand and slapped his right palm on the counter.

"That's me," I confirmed.

"Man, my bad for my crassness. I didn't know that was you. I was just trying to engage you for a tip," he apologized.

"Young blood, it's cool because it's me. Just be careful because there are a lot companies that hire secret customers to check on employees."

"I'm Bernard, but my people call me B. Smoov--no *e*. I make beats," he said while reaching in his back pocket to retrieve something.

"Well, B. Smoov, keep your focus on your work so you don't get called out."

"Yeh! Yeh! But uh, do you think you can listen to my CD for some feedback? I'm trying to get out of this gig so I can go to New York City to make some dough. I'm trying to be the next Puffy."

"Why not be the next B. Smoov?" I asked and sipped.

"I don't get it." He was puzzled.

"Tell you what...if you go back to school and are serious about your craft, I'll help you. My number won't ever change." I gave B. Smoov my card and turned my back to him to signal I was done talking.

The thought crossed my mind to go look for Mel, but I didn't want to press the issue. I put the ball in her hand to reach out to me. I tipped B. Smoov; he handed me a bottled water and gestured it was on the house. I put an extra $50 in his hand and said, "Go re-apply, bruh."

A half-step away from the bar, the smell of Haiku caressed my nose. There was only one person I knew who rejected high-end perfumes and stuck with the Avon brand. Mel was near. The scent wafted closer to me. Then, there was a tap on my shoulder.

"You all finished at the bar?" she asked.

"I guess so."

CARAMEL'S SUNDAY

We just both smiled at each other. The miles of conversations that could be had in that moment were endless. I didn't want to ruin the moment, so I asked Caramel for a dance. In that instant, the bass guitar strummed the beginning of *She Used to Be My Girl* by the O'Jays.

My Mel Caramel smiled and laughed as she accepted my hand leading her to the dance floor.

The lights dimmed in the room. The lights in Mel's eyes sparkled. I shut up long enough to listen to the time we missed as the soundtracks from the past, present, and future played for us.

CARAMEL'S SUNDAY

SLEEP STAGE 4
Don't Wake Me...

This is the deepest and most restorative sleep. Muscles are relaxed, energy is restored, and hormones are released for growth and regeneration.
                    -The National Sleep Foundation

CARAMEL'S SUNDAY

JPEG 015
Networking in a Wet Dream on Dry Ice

The secret was out. I danced in public. There were three people in the world who saw me dance: Aunt Maggs, who whupped my butt so hard when she saw me dancing to Salt-N-Pepa's *Shake Your Thang*--"The devil in hell will not have you!" she screamed while tearing my *thang* up in my bedroom-- Dolly, who caught me jamming to Bobby Brown's *My Prerogative* when she came to visit in Garysburg the same summer--"OOOH! I'm telling Aunt Maggs you lettin' the devil in here," I shut her up by giving her my collection of refunding, recycle bottles--and lastly, I danced with Solomon, in my dorm room one night when I had a relapse thinking of my parents and how I felt like my life was not catching up to the plans of my classmates. He held me while I cried to Michael Jackson's *You Are Not Alone*. Then he made me groove to Marvin Gaye's *Gotta Give It Up!*

"Aunt Maggs ain't around. So you can grind on me if you want," he said jokingly. The countless times we dry humped was too painful for both of us that we opted out of grinding on the dance floor. As silly as it sounds, Solomon was willing to wait to fully consummate our union while we dated.

"You have some moves, woman. I can wait," he'd say.

"What are you going to do in the meantime?" I asked.

"I am a pretty patient man."

"Yeh, but what about *Thor?*" That's what we called his male parts.

"As long as your sunshine waits for me, I can keep the hammer under control."

Jeffrey Banks stole a few steps with me before excusing himself to converse with some investors. Shelly was getting her groove on during the rotation of the line dances and never came back to her seat. As I looked around, I saw Solomon standing by himself at the bar, and was hesitant about asking him to dance, but I figured, what the hell. He paid for the dress. He might as well get something out of it after all these years. Out of the corner of my eye, Shelly was vigorously giving me the thumbs-up from the dance floor. She was dancing with some stuffed-shirt. I thought he would have a heart attack when she backed her booty up on him.

"Do you want to dance?" I got up the courage to ask. I was glad he didn't turn me away.

"Why not?" Solomon extended his arm to escort me to the dance floor.

Even with the passing of four years, his embrace still felt comforting. I remembered his arms always feeling like home.

"I see you haven't stopped wearing Haiku," Solomon said while removing a loose curl from my face.

"You noticed," I replied.

"I also see someone is not as shy and reserved as she used to be about dancing in public," Solomon said while pulling me closer to him when The O'Jays sang, *If I had the chance, I'd take her back.*

Solomon was a natural flirt, but had an overwhelming sense of self-control.

The beat dropped for Marvin Gaye's *Gotta Give It Up.* I was almost convinced Solomon paid the band for their selection of music.

"Did you set this up, man?' I asked, laughing.

Solomon released me, put both his hands up, and said, "I swear to God! I didn't, Mel! It is rather funny, though. Right?" His hand in mine, we began to two-step.

"Yeh. It sure is."

We only grooved for three songs, but it felt like an eternity. I thought my feet would be hurting, but I guess

I was having so much fun that nothing mattered.

As the band transitioned to a new song, Solomon whispered, "Call me. For real, Mel. We need to talk."

I nodded in agreement.

Solomon disappeared into the crowd until I found him chopping it up with Tonya. They seemed really buddy-buddy. I couldn't be mad if Thor had found his leading lady since I left Solomon. Could I? All this dressing up and reminiscing took me out of character, but it sure felt good. It was like warm chocolate on a cold day. It felt like I was coming on my period.

I frantically looked for Shelly. She was handling business at one of the rear tables. Her laptop was out, she was talking with that Shelly-Royal-confidence. I slid the shoes off because I could now feel the impact of them from my dancing. I shuffled my way through the crowd to walk the perimeter of the board room with my legs very close together.

Talking through my teeth, I said, "Shelly, I have an emergency."

"Excuse me, Mr. Freeman."

Shelly joined me in the corner of the room.

"Girl, what's going on? I was about to close on an opportunity to help this gentleman revamp the brand of his barbershop."

"Sorry, girl, but I think I just started my cycle. I don't have any pads."

"...and you know I'm always prepared. Gimme two minutes. Let me wrap this up."

"Hurry. This night is seemingly perfect; I don't want to ruin it."

"Okay. Okay."

Shelly really did mean two minutes. She shook hands with the man and grabbed me to make a quick trip to the restroom.

Oddly, we were the only people in the restroom. Shelly talked to me through the stall.

"So? Did it come on?"

I was silent.

"Mel!" Shelly yelled.

I slowly opened the door and looked at her with a weird expression.

"Girl, say something!"

"I don't really know what to say. It was clear."

"Clear? Hmm." Shelly placed her balled fists on her hip. Then a light bulb went off in her head.

"Was it sticky? I know you touched it, Curious Georgina."

"I did. It was."

Another small moment of silence filled the room. Then the revelation hit her.

Wide-eyed, Shelly shouted, "Oh, my God! You're horny! It all makes sense. I saw you and Solomon on the dance floor getting cozy."

"Shut up, Shelly!" I tried to silence her while looking around even though I knew we were alone.

Her eyebrows danced up and down. "Caramel. It's time. You're 29. Break the seal. Solomon is all there is to talk about in the entertainment industry."

"He is?" I asked.

"Duh! Yeh! Don't you keep up with *Variety* magazine?"

"I subscribe, but I don't see any pictures of Solomon in there."

"See, that's your problem. You're focused on pictures and not details in the text. My goodness. C'mon, girl. Eww...wait, wash your hands first," Shelly cautioned me.

While I washed my hands, Shelly shouted expletives about me being almost 30 and not knowing the difference between my period flowing and lady juice in my panties. I was guilty. Suppression is sexual ignorance.

"It just ain't damn normal! Let's get out of here 'fo I pop a vein. Yo' Aunt Maggs shoulda talked about the scripture that mentioned tasting fruit and orgasms."

"Ain't no such scripture, Shells!" I plucked her.

"Well, there should be. Geesh!" The door of the restroom closed and we quickly composed ourselves.

Shelly's fussing and cussing had me wondering if Solomon had been celibate since our break-up. He wasn't a virgin, or at least I assumed he wasn't because he dated a few girls from his elite group of friends. Mr. Montgomery arranged for Solomon to meet girls from his wealthy network of friends. Solomon would always joke and say "Rich girls looking for trust-fund dudes put out like you wouldn't believe." I would kindly remind him that I wasn't rich and I wasn't *putting out*. By my definition, French kissing while wearing only my bra and bottoms was as much putting out that I had done as an adult. The occasional dry hump was too painful, so I just opted to keep my virtue until I had time to deal with the consequences, positive or negative, that came along with sex. Salt-N-Pepa continued to echo in my head; they were my most reliable sources.

Upon entering the ballroom, a lovely treat greeted us. Both Jeffrey and Solomon stood laughing and talking with Tonya. Jeffrey saw me mid-laugh and flagged me down to come near him. Solomon turned to see who was coming, and he just grinned.

Shelly and I looked at each other. My eyes told her she was coming with me. Solomon recognized her and eased up on the attention to me. We moved in unison, Shelly and I.

"Solomon, Tonya, this is Caramel Moss, CEO of E.Y.E., Inc." While extending my hand to Tonya, he then noticed I had company. "...and I haven't had the pleasure of meeting this young lady."

"Shelly Royal. It's a pleasure to meet you, Tonya! Hey, Solomon!" They embraced.

"Oh, you know each other," Jeffrey said adjusting his tuxedo jacket.

"Yes, we all know each other. We went to the same high school in..." Solomon couldn't finish his sentence. Jeffrey interrupted with a snap of his finger.

"Garysburg! Right?"

"Very good, Mr. Banks. That's our hometown."

"Hmm. Interesting. Well, I tell you what. Because we're all friends, I'm having a night cap at my house in Morewood before flying out. All of you should come over."

"Morewood Estates? Mr. Banks, I thought you lived in Virginia," I inquired.

He winked at me, "That's just one of my properties."

"As gracious as a host I know you'll be, Mr. Banks, I have to take your niece around for some more promotional events this evening. I promise to have her back at a decent hour," Solomon said.

"Caramel? Shelly?" Mr. Banks looked to us for an answer.

"I was feeling a bit uncomfortable and reached with my eyes for Shelly to give one of her great PR responses."

"I can't make it this trip. My flight for Chicago leaves early in the morning. Caramel don't you have a shoot early tomorrow?" Shelly chimed in.

"Actually, Jeffrey, I do have an early morning shoot. We're still on for next week, right?" Jeffrey grabbed my hand and kissed the back of it.

"We are, indeed, my lady." Jeffrey said.

I blushed a bit and tried not to make eye contact with Solomon.

"You ladies enjoy the rest of the fundraiser. I have to get back to my villa. Tonya, it was good seeing you, baby, and Hug your parents for me." Jeffrey kissed his niece on the cheek. Then, he extended his hand to Solomon, in preparation for a farewell handshake.

"Well, Banks, we better get out of here. I'll catch up with you about that thing another time," Solomon said.

Solomon said his final goodbyes to Shelly and me, hugging and slightly lifting Shelly off the floor. He squeezed me a bit tighter and said, "Check in with ya, later, Mel."

The light of the evening ended and seemed to fade to black, but with both gentlemen out of the way, I had no more distractions and could concentrate on networking.

Shelly was excited to introduce me to Roger Freeman, a barbershop owner who was looking to franchise in other major urban areas throughout the U.S. Just before I interrupted their meeting, she had mentioned that she would recommend me to develop a photo montage of his business's philanthropy efforts for his web page to encourage his investors.

"I told him giving back to the community was your specialty," she updated me as we moved toward Mr. Freeman.

"Thanks, girl," I said with the utmost gratitude.

"When I come up the ranks, you come up the ranks," Shelly encouraged.

CARAMEL'S SUNDAY

Having mentioned Mr. Freeman's philanthropy, I recalled reading an article of a local businessman who donated a percentage from each paying customer's bill toward academic scholarships for four high-achieving students in under-resourced neighborhoods and four students from more privileged communities with more than 1000 hours of documented community service in D.C. In the 10 years Mr. Freeman has been in business, he and his customers supported 80 students who committed themselves to finishing their undergraduate education. I could live with working for an organization that supports students and their dreams.

"Here we go," Shelly beamed with excitement just 10 paces from Mr. Freeman; and go, we did. Shelly's pitch to represent him as a client was so phenomenal that Mr. Freeman disregarded the fact that she lived more than 700 miles away. Remote access was Shelly's specialty. She could write a press release about someone better than for whom she was writing it. Shelly had a gift of absorbing the energy of a project or a client in order to present them in the best light, distract an audience from a folly, or make readers forgive, all together, a wrong her client committed. She was great! With that said, Mr. Freeman hired me to capture the new brand of Freeman's Barbershop, nation-wide.

With a connection to Mr. Freeman, I could expand my business and continue to market my work privately and commercially. Just after wrapping up with Mr. Freeman, Shelly connected me with a few more friends in her circle. By the end of the night, I had exchanged cards with more than 20 possible clients. It was clear that life truly had its ups and downs. There was no need to wake me from my dreams. I was on the move; however, there was one question that needed to be answered. Who would ride this cloud with me besides my best friend? Curiosity was calling. I had hoped it wouldn't kill the cat.

CARAMEL'S SUNDAY

JPEG 016
Back at Ben's

CARAMEL'S SUNDAY

I was in mid-dial when Solomon's number appeared on the face of my phone. I didn't answer it. I waited a moment and then decided to call him. He asked me to make the move. Maybe it was a butt-dial. Either way, I didn't want to seem anxious. Besides, I really did need to be careful with my thoughts. I didn't want to get caught off-guard. I was, oddly, a bit nervous. I wouldn't bother Miss E. with this one. I'd handle it on my own. Well, the truth was neither Miss E., Dolly, nor Shelly answered their cells in between my call back to Solomon. I had to put on my big girl panties.

He let the phone ring 20 times before he answered. No, wait, that was my imagination and recall of New Edition's *Mr. Telephone Man*. It was more like five rings.

"Mel, Caramel! What's good, young lady?" he said with some indistinct chatter in the background.

"I'm good, Sol," I replied.

I grabbed my camera lenses and began to clean them to keep my hands busy. Air blower. Check. Camel hair brush. Check. Micro-fiber cloth. Check. Alcohol. Check.

It was clear he was talking with someone. Who? I wasn't sure.

"If you're busy, I can call later," I encouraged.

"No! No! You're straight. Look, have you eaten breakfast?"

"Solomon, it's four in the afternoon?"

"Well, by breakfast I mean lunch. Industry time reference is a little off." Solomon chuckled at our different perspectives of time.

"I haven't. Are you asking me out for lunch?"

"Only if you're free." He didn't impose.

"I'm free. Should I meet you some place?"

"You won't believe this, but I'm at Ben's doing a promotion. Everyone from Tonya's camp will clear out in about 30 minutes. Can you make it here?"

Really, Solomon? Ben's? The universe had a really interesting way of bringing us back together. I played along.

"Sure. Why not?" I said. I'll be there in an hour. You can order me a..."

"Half smoke--split, with grilled onions, relish, and mustard on a toasted bun, coleslaw instead of chips, and a bottled water," Solomon interrupted.

"You remembered?" I asked.

"I never forgot. See you in an hour," he said.

Before the exchange about my order, I was headed to my closet to pull out the same hooded sweatshirt with the rhinestone camera on it and a pair of jeans. I planned to put my hair in a ponytail to resemble the last time I looked at Ben's back in 2002. It was in that moment that I understood why guys hated when girls played games. I was in my feelings about where we were having lunch thinking Solomon was playing games. Then I considered, *Maybe it was just the universe--again--circling back so we could do things differently.*

While I was still more drawn to a relaxed look, I kept my hair down, wore a white short-sleeved wrap around shirt, fitted jeans, and a pair of open-toed sandals. My French manicure was still good, so I had to show it off. I threw on a knitted cardigan in case it became breezy. It was still spring. In D.C., that could also mean autumn.

It would have been easier for me to take Metro, but it was faster for me to drive. Then I thought about rush hour traffic and parking and decided to call a cab. That would delay my arrival by a few minutes. I called to update Solomon.

"Take your time. I'll be here," he said calmly.

During the cab ride to Ben's, Dolly calls. Perfect.

"Girl, what's up? I was at my last fitting for the," she said with breathiness.

"I'm meeting Solomon for lunch."

"You mean like right now, right now?"

"I mean like I'm in a cab on my way to Ben's Chili Bowl, right now." I enlarged my eyes as I spoke to her while emphasizing my words. I knew she couldn't see me, but I had hope Dolly could hear the inflection in my voice.

"Yeh! Try that one."

"Huh?" I asked.

"Oh. No. I was talking to Cita. She's having a wardrobe malfunction with her dress."

"I see."

"I wish you liked this sort of thing, but I'm glad you'll be taking my behind the scene pics."

"Yeh, me, too. Maybe you'll inspire me to make it one of my things." I couldn't believe I even mouthed the insinuation.

"So, wait, back to you. You're going to have lunch with Mr. Solomon Montgomery Brooks. Wow! How do you feel about that?" Dolly inquired.

"I don't know. I guess I'm okay with it. You know that first encounter since the break-up made me feel something new," I chuckled at the thought. Dolly burst into laughter.

"Girl, you had me in tears! I can't believe..." I interrupted her.

"I know. I know. Shush! So, what if it happens again."

"Well did you start your cycle?"

"No."

"Then you'll know. It's a natural body response. You might even enjoy it this time around," Dolly said.

"Okay, so what if he brings up the break-up?"

"He might, but be cool about it. You were both younger. If he's still holding on to it and is planning some scheme to get back at you, then be glad you left that pettiness four years ago."

"Doll, he's been so sweet. He's...he's like the best friend I remember from Garysburg."

"Caramel, stop tripping and enjoy yourself. I always liked Solomon. He's a good dude. Just be cool. Ooh, Lawd! Cita's butt won't let the dress zip all the way up. I gotta go. Don't forget the rehearsal dinner in two weeks."

Before I could tell her I would remember, Dolly was gone.

The cabby was kind enough to pretend he wasn't listening to me, but the grin on his face suggested that he caught a part of my discussion. When we arrived at

Ben's, I paid my fare, and the cabby looked at me and said, "Best friends are forever." Then he gave me a head nod to alert me that I wasn't alone. Solomon stood waiting for me to get out of the cab. I moved out of the way. He closed the door then ran to open another one.

CARAMEL'S SUNDAY

JPEG 017
The Moment When Time Grows Up...

"Hey, Jay! I'm ready for that order. Thanks, man!" Solomon said to a man on the grill. The man named Jay gave Solomon a head nod as I was ushered to the back of Ben's Chili Bowl as patrons standing in the line gave me the side-eye. They waited as I anticipated what conversation would be in store for Solomon and me.

As always, Solomon was a gentleman; he pulled out my chair. I looked around expecting to see new decor inside of Ben's, but that was wishful thinking. Part of its niche was an atmosphere of a sit-down, community diner. The autographed pictures of local and national figures served as wallpaper from the front to back of Ben's. Just above my head was a picture of Tres Chain E. and Solomon.

"This seat was intentional, huh?" I asked.

"You know me, Mel. Everything I do has a purpose," he said.

"Well, what's the purpose for this seating arrangement?"

"If you look closer, you'll see a full circle."

I looked closer and couldn't put my finger on it until I caught a glimpse of my hoodie. It was from the last time Solomon and I were together.

"But..." I tried to come up with something to say.

"Just when you walked out the door, Tres grabbed me for a quick picture. Once he had it developed, he brought it back and signed it for the Wall of Fame," Solomon explained.

"If you hadn't brought us back here, I would have missed it."

"I know."

"Oh, really? You think you know me, but..."

"Mel, it's my job to study people and patterns. I just had a lapse in judgment when I got comfortable with you. For that, I am very sorry."

Solomon pulled his hand from under the table, grabbed mine, and looked me in the eyes with the sincerest of apologies. Here I was thinking I would extend the courtesy for my lack of decorum when sending an email instead of talking things out. All I could do is swallow a little spittle and ask for something to drink. In that moment, our food came to the table.

I reached for my purse to get the hand sanitizer when I heard the top of one open in Solomon's hands.

"See, I told you I know you."

"Well, I was actually grabbing my purse to go to the ladies room to use warm water and soap."

Solomon laughed, closed the cap, and said, "Well, I guess I can be wrong this once."

I lied, and got up to do as I said--wash my hands and get my mind together.

It bothered me that Solomon wasn't upset, didn't give me the cold shoulder, or even hint that the past was the past. He just picked up where we left off but with a game stronger than I had ever encountered. It was without a filter. He was playing spades with an open hand. I exposed everything.

Questions lingered: What has he been doing all this time? With whom has he been doing them? Why is he pursuing something that was wrecked in the past? I was just confused.

I got myself together, put on a little gloss--not sure why because I was about to devour the half-smoke sandwich. I was actually a little nervous and off-guard. Either way, this was happening. By this, I meant a possible chance at redemption, a clean slate. I had to stay focused since my career was taking a new turn and I would possibly have some new long-term contracts.

"Come on, girl. Get it together. It's just Solomon. You're Caramel Moss. Stick to your strength," I whispered to myself.

179

CARAMEL'S SUNDAY

Back at our private trip down memory lane, Solomon stood as I approached the table.

"Sol, you know you don't have to do that. It's me."

"But don't I? I'm saying, it is my reintroduction to you. Two worlds, not one," he said.

"Let's just bless this food."

"Absolutely."

Solomon knew that I liked unbroken circles. He extended both his hands, freshly covered in hand sanitizer. He also knew I was a bit compulsive about hygiene.

"Father, thank you for this reunion of old friends, in a familiar place, with renewed spirits. Thank you for the food we're 'bout to receive for the nourishment of our bodies in Christ name we pray, Amen."

"Amen."

We both dug into our lunches.

"Still like your chili burger and chili dog at the same time, huh?" I asked.

"There's no other way, lady."

We sat in silence until our plates were nearly clean. He didn't pressure me for conversation. I liked that. I enjoyed setting the tone. It kept me from having to fish for things to say.

"So besides managing beautiful models, what else is new?"

"What? You don't read *Variety*?" Solomon joked.

"You sound like Shelly," I responded.

"Well, she would know. She's the hottest PR agent in Chicago."

"I try not to get involved in all that news," I said.

"I'm not telling you what to do, but it does help you stay abreast of what's trending in the industry."

"Are you on Facebook or Twitter?"

"Face what? Twit huh?"

"Oh, man! Mel! I'm going to have to school you on the latest. Soon, print media is going to be obsolete. The digital world is taking over. I hate to tell you this, but even art is going to take a turn with a high digital presence."

"You're evading my original question," I warned.

Solomon took a napkin to his face to get off the excess chili and then wiped his hand.

"It wasn't my intent. Let me respond, I'm managing Tonya and one other model. My hands are still in the music business. I have a team now, so, I don't have to hustle as much. They find talent for me, I consider them for the labels, and I pitch them to be signed."

"So you're not with a label at all?" I asked.

"No, I'm more like an agent. I get my money off the top. I'm not into chasing people down for my cash. A client gets a deal, I get my cut. If they want additional representation, we're talking retainer fees."

"So you feed the industry writers, bands, solo artists and then let them assume all the liability?"

"Don't forget, I manage models, too, Mel Caramel!"

Solomon popped two cheese covered fries into his mouth and gave me a wink.

"Wow! What does Mr. Montgomery have to say about all this?"

"Honestly..." He takes a swig of his soda. "He's not as upset about my choice anymore. He sees I'm holding my own, and that's all that matters."

"So who is he grooming for the business? Angela?"

"Yup. It's in her blood. She really loves it. From time to time, we brainstorm ideas for product marketing for the barbecue sauces and Brooks grocery line of meats."

"So the jingles for the commercials..."

"My artists..." Solomon gloated.

"Checks and mo' checks."

"Speaking of checks, I saw *Capitol Offense* in New York."

"Yeh, about that?" I lowered my eyes because I knew he knew that was our picture.

"So, where's my cut for my part in the photo?"

"Huh?" I played dumb.

"If you can 'huh,' you can hear, woman."

"Well, what had happened was..."

"Yeh! I bet." Solomon cut his eyes at me.

While I knew Solomon was partially joking about his cut for the photo, I did feel a little guilty about not thinking to include a cut for him. His image was in it, but his face wasn't showing. So, I figured I was in the clear.

Our lunch date was surprisingly pleasant. We were on a neutral plane. The air was cleared at the beginning. I still felt compelled to throw my apology on the table.

"Sol, I apologize for not taking a more mature approach...you know with the break-up and all."

"No apology necessary."

My phone buzzed in my pocket. I was ready to dismiss it, but it continued after the first rotation of rings. I placed it on silent.

"You don't want to get that?" Solomon inquired.

"Naw, I'm good."

"Wow!"

"Wow, what?"

"I'm worthy of your time is all."

"Solomon, I find it rude to be on a call or to even pick up a call while entertaining company. You know that."

"...but you don't even want to know who you're ignoring?"

"If it's important, a message or text will be left."

"See! That's what I miss about you." Again with the hand-holding. I didn't fight it, but I did wonder why it was so frequent.

Solomon lived in New York. I wasn't moving from the D.C. area any time soon. I am glad I didn't have emotions that couldn't be contained. Being with Solomon felt good, but I knew it was just for the afternoon. Would we see each other again? Maybe, once in a while, we could connect after my Wednesday shoots in New York. If he visited Maryland, I could give him a tour of my favorite places. Even still, Solomon just kept me wondering where this lunch was going to go.

I slithered my hand slowly from his grasp so we could return to neutral ground. I didn't want to move too fast.

"Too much?" he asked.

"Not too much, it's just that it's..."

"It's weird, huh? Connecting after so many years of silence, things are supposed to be awkward, not back to normal. I get it."

"Well, yeh! I don't see how you've been able to be so cool about things after the way I left them." I found myself whining.

Solomon cleared his throat, leaned in closer to me, and just stared.

"Mel, I've loved you since the moment I met you. Period. All I ever did was try to love you more and more."

"I don't know love, like LOVE, love Sol. I loved you like family and enough to marry you because we would be family, but the emotions tied to love left when Mom and Dad died," I said.

"Even with that, Mel, I didn't care about emotions, you just gave me you. You never wanted anything, and you didn't put me in a box as the rich kid who had it all. You just loved me. With a love like that, I never had to wonder where your loyalties lay. I never had to try to impress you. You didn't fall for anything. Up front, cards on the table...That was...is you. Most people won't get that."

"Yeh, but you did try to impart a little of you on me. I just didn't get down with that, Sol. I change when I feel like it, not because of pressure," I said.

"If your leaving me had to remind me of that, I welcomed it. It felt shitty at first, but I got it later. What was it you said to me when I questioned you about doing more than just taking pictures and drawing?"

I laughed. He went to a place of sensitivity.

"My dreams are real..."

"Right...'just because you can't see them doesn't mean they are impossible to achieve.'"

"Yeh. That was it." I laughed.

"I was becoming more like my old man, Mel...challenging you to be something you weren't."

"Mm hmm," I sounded out the letters clearly. I reached over and took two of his remaining fries off his plate and ate them. That was my way of accepting his surrender to letting me be me.

Solomon pulled out his cell, held up one finger, and started dialing. He smiled as he held the phone to his ear.

CARAMEL'S SUNDAY

"Ben, it's Solomon. Look, I need you to handle my clients I have for the rest of the week. I'll be back in New York on Sunday night. Yeh, you got this. Thanks."

We sat in silence for what seemed like five minutes, until my phone alerted me with more buzzing. I looked down and saw the light on my phone inside my purse. A text appeared shortly after:

Jeffrey Banks
I can't wait for our dinner next week.

CARAMEL'S SUNDAY

JPEG 018
The Red Doors

Solomon cleared his schedule for me--for a week. Either he was trying to make up for lost time and make good on a promise that he would be the one to deflower me, or he was serious about loving me since the first time we met. Solomon was playing for keeps.

Because I had not found a full-time job, my schedule was wide open, except for my weekly commitment to be in New York and volunteering in Garysburg on Sunday. After explaining that I had to be on the set in Brooklyn for the Ace's Cheesecakes shoot, Solomon agreed to hang in my shadows while he watched me work for a change.

"I'll even ride the train with you," he decided.

"Well, that would mean we'd both have to get up pretty early. I already wake up at 4 to get on the road to catch the train out of Union Station," I told him.

"Well, I'll check out of the Hilton and get two rooms closer to the station so we can sleep."

"Two rooms?" I inquired.

"Two rooms. You know how much I respect you waiting until our wedding night," Solomon said matter-of-factly.

"That's quite presumptuous of you. Who says I haven't already *given it up?*" I winked at him, unconvincingly.

"Yeh, I'd know, Mel. Trust me." Solomon was secure in his response. He was right, but I left the subject at hand alone.

Ordinarily, I would reject the offer of letting him pay for a room for me, but who turns down a few extra winks of sleep on someone else's dime? It was settled.

"So, what do you want to do this week?"

"I'm game for whatever. Surprise me."

"Who are you? Since when do you like surprises?" he asked.

"Since today. I figure since you're going the extra mile, I would change things up a bit, too." I didn't know what I was getting into, but it felt strange and good. A little bit of Miss E. must have been running through my veins.

"Alright then. Let's start with something simple. How about we catch a movie and get some ice cream afterward?"

"Banana split with caramel, chocolate, and strawberry sauce?" I asked.

"As you wish."

"You know I like independent films."

"So it sounds like we're headed to Eastern Market," Solomon suggested.

Eastern Market was the location of an independent film theater. We had been a few times during our long-distance relationship. While mainstream theater whet Solomon's palette, I could appreciate the hard work put into a very costly venture. Gregorio started out as an indie film maker. He caught the attention of a few investors, and his films were picked up by more affluent distributors. He was the Martin Scorsese of indie films for my generation--even If I were the only fan in my circle. I imagine *Capitol Offense* was Solomon's favorite for obvious reasons.

Monday was the movies and ice cream. Tuesday night, we enjoyed a visit to an art exhibition by my friends Baba Ski and Vince Love. They partnered on a project called, *The Faces of Change*. They explored the evolution of the residents in D.C. who transitioned from poverty to wealth through education, entrepreneurship, and, in some cases, being in the right place at the right time. There was an entire series of D.C. *Black Broadway*--U Street. Of course, Ben's was a part of it.

"We just can't get away from this place, huh?" Solomon joked."

Wednesday was an interesting day of events. I wasn't use to Solomon taking a back seat to my life. As promised, he made a reservation for me to stay at a hotel close to Union Station.

"Don't drive. Catch a cab, I'll take care of the tab when you arrive."

"What am I going to do for transportation when I'm there?" I asked.

"I hijacked your week, so I'm responsible for it. If you want to pay me back once you pick up a long-term gig, I'll cash the check. In the meantime, chill, Mel! I got you. No strings attached."

I followed his instruction. It was pretty nice not to be rushed in the morning to make it to New York City. It was also nice not to have to pressure Solomon to rise earlier than his schedule required.

"Are you going to check into your office while we're up there?"

"Having a mobile office makes life easier. If Ben needs me, he'll reach out. Besides, I think Tonya likes working with him more than me. They have a crush on each other, but neither will admit it."

"Isn't that a conflict of interest?" I asked

"You know it, but wasn't my barter to work with my father on the days he came to Garysburg a conflict of, too? I trained Ben to keep the business separate from his ambitions to *hit it*."

I punched Solomon in the arm.

"What? I'm just being real about it!" He rubbed his arm to relax the slight pain.

The train ride up was peaceful. Because it was still early, there were few distractions. Most riders were either reading the paper, listening to music on their MP3 Players or iPods, or sleeping. I scrolled through my Blackberry for the weather until I fell asleep. I woke up to the last sound of my snoring as the trained pulled into Penn Station.

"Wake up, sleepy head." Solomon slid me off his arm.

"I was gone, huh?"

"Pretty much! Get your things."

Once we hit 34th Street, Solomon hailed us a cab to take to Brooklyn. With all of my equipment, I was glad I had the extra hands to help.

When we entered the doors of Deuce's, a woman screamed. She rushed to hug Solomon and kissed him on the lips!

"Oh, my Gosh! You are here! Did you hear? Did you hear?" the woman yelled loudly.

Solomon looked over at me with an awkward glance.

"Jessica! Hey! Did I hear what?" he asked.

"I'm the cover model for Deuce's new cheesecake print ad. Ben called me this morning at 5 a.m. Apparently, the model that was originally booked is now two months pregnant and throwing up all over the place. She cancelled at one in the morning. Bad for her, good for me."

"Mel, Jessica. Jessica, Mel!"

"Oh! I'm sorry." Jessica forced her hand in mine and began to shake it vigorously.

"Hi, Jessica!"

"Is this your sister?" she asked.

"No, my sister is Angela. This is Mel..." he seemed to search for a title to give me. I didn't want to blow up his spot, so I interjected.

"I'm the photographer who will be shooting you today, but hair and makeup doesn't start until noon. Why are you here so early?"

"Nerves, I guess. I didn't want to be late. I hadn't had a gig in a year until I started working with Solly! He's the greatest."

"Oh! Okay. Good," I said with a forced smile.

"Mel, I'm going to get us some coffee and tea. Do your thing. If you need me, let me know."

I didn't think it was possible for Solomon to be comfortable not being in charge or at the center of making magic happen, but he really let me do my *thing,* as he said. He watched, smiled, scrolled through messages on his phone, dropped a few bottles of water beside me, and just let me be. It was refreshing. I was on assignment, but the ad agency let me call the shots. They trusted my vision.

"You're damn good at what you do, Mel! I am impressed."

"Did you doubt me?" I asked.

"No. I didn't doubt you, but I stood still long enough to notice. I'm catching up to your speed."

"Well, I appreciate that. Let me finish up with the agency, and then we can start packing up."

"Why don't you pass me your equipment and I'll pack up what I can," Solomon offered.

"You don't know where my things go," I countered.

"How hard could it be to put cameras and lights back in bags?"

"Please, just follow the colored labels. Do know that none of it is cheap and will cost you if you break any of the pieces," I warned.

I signed some documents, got my check, and headed back to the front of Ace's Cheesecakes where I saw Solomon waiting for me.

"It's breakfast time," he said.

"You mean lunch or dinner time," I said.

"Same thing. C'mon, I'm treating, today," Solomon noted, slyly.

"You always treat, Sol," I said with a grin.

After making sure I had all my things, we hailed a cab to travel to Solomon's apartment in West Harlem. He rented a loft because he didn't want to make a 30-year investment in a place he knew he wasn't going to call home. Oddly enough, he made plans to retire in Richmond when he was tired of the entertainment business.

"Do you think you'll ever go back to the food business?"

"Dad would like that, wouldn't he?"

"I'm sure he would. You're his only son. He has to feel a little on the outside seeing his brothers and their sons continuing the family legacy."

It appeared that the subject was a sore spot for Solomon. He evaded and just started talking about how beautiful the country side is in the spring.

"We're going to pick up my car and then drive up to Milton."

"Where's Milton?"

"It's a town upstate. I have a buddy up there who lets me use his cabin from time to time."

"Are you sure it's available at the last minute?"

"What do you think I was doing while you were working?"

"Duh! Paying attention to my work flow!"

"Yeh! That too. It's cool. He's not using it."

Solomon had the day planned for us. I was excited about traveling upstate and didn't even think to consider the fact that we might spend the night. I was sure Solomon wouldn't have me in a compromising position, but I wouldn't put it past him. He was, after all, still a man.

I kept silent on the ride to his apartment, playing Salt-N-Pepa's greatest hits while scrolling through the shots I took at Ace's. I wasn't being rude, I was being committed.

"You're going to miss all the sites of the big city," Solomon said.

"You know skylines don't impress me," I said.

"True, but I know what will."

"Excuse me, sir?" I plucked his arm.

"Just wait and see."

Solomon was good about not bothering me for the rest of the cab ride. He told me we'd have about two hours in the car in route to Milton. By the time I got through the raw photos, we were at Solomon's apartment. I put my camera back in its case and waited for Solomon to let me out of the cab.

I stretched and yawned at the same time. I noticed, just as my eyes opened, that I was in front of my old building when Solomon and I first moved to New York City--The Alexis Apartments and Suites. Solomon flicked my lips.

"Stop looking surprised, Mel," he said.

"I'm just saying. You're such a creature of habit."

Solomon laughed. "I am a creature of saving money. Just because I have it doesn't mean I need to spend it. Come on!"

The driver slammed the trunk shut as he handed us my bags. There was nothing more for me to do but enjoy this journey. It was like watching my life in reverse but with a more keen eye and a grown-up attitude. The same doorman was on post. I couldn't believe it.

"Hey, Ralph."

Ralph tipped his hat and gave me a smile at the same time he gave Solomon a glance.

"Miss Caramel. It's good to see you."

I extended my arms for a hug. Ralph cut his eyes at Solomon.

Ralph reached out to give me a squeeze. "See, I told you she really loved me, little buddy!"

"Go ahead, man!" Solomon popped a mint in his mouth and waited for me to finish hugging Ralph.

Ralph, in his late 50s, would always joke with Solomon about taking me away from him because only older men could take care of delicate ladies. I saw Solomon take a quick look at his watch and decided to cut my conversation short.

"I hope to see you more Miss Caramel," Ralph yelled quickly as I disappeared through the glass double doors.

"I can't believe Ralph is still here."

"I know, right. The more things change..."

"Don't! Please don't cliché me, boy!"

CARAMEL'S SUNDAY

The elevator opened as soon as we approached it. I went to press the number 10 until Solomon stopped me.

"Top floor, now, baby!"

"Oh! Fancy, are we?"

"Same building, new unit. I work hard," Solomon said.

Solomon planned to drop off his dirty laundry and pack a new set of clothes. I wasn't quite sure what I was going to do, seeing that I usually catch the train back home from my shoot. Knowing Solomon, he might actually still have some of my old clothes in his drawer. I'd be a bit concerned that he held on to them so long, but I'd be glad to change clothes because I felt a little clammy after perspiring a bit at the shoot. I anticipated the next moments of my escapades with Solomon Montgomery Brooks as we ascended to the 20th floor.

Buzz! Buzz! It was a text message from Dolly. I knew the closer she got to her nuptials, I'd hear from her more often.

Cousin Dolly
When are you getting home from NY?

Me
Umm...tomorrow, maybe.

CARAMEL'S SUNDAY

Cousin Dolly
TOMORROW! I need a quick headshot for my new business cards. What's going up there?

Me
Can't promise you. And...umm...huh???

Dolly
Violet Caramel Moss! Are you okay? Stop playing.

Me
I'm fine. With Solomon.

My phone rang; it was Dolly. I braced myself for a high-pitched, anxious woman on the other end of the phone. Before answering the call, I decided to send her to voicemail. She wasn't used to that.

Buzz! Buzz! She didn't waste any time trying to call me for the dirt.

Dolly
Heifer! Don't send me to voicemail. What is going on, fresh tail?

Me
Oh! This and that.

Dolly
This and that, hell! You call me as soon as you're free doing God knows what!

Me
It's no different than what you and Gerald did that one time!

CARAMEL'S SUNDAY

Dolly
Smart tail! Call me! Seriously, don't do nothing crazy before telling me.

Me
I promise (giggles).

Bing! "We're here," Solomon alerted.

The elevator opened and my eyes widened. Solomon was right, he did know what would impress me. His apartment walls were adorned with my artwork. It was cataloged from senior year photographs to artwork I completed at the turn of the century. The pieces were displayed in reverse order of their creation. Solomon walked ahead of me as if no commentary was necessary. I was in complete disbelief.

"There is some promotional gear in the room to the right--underwear included! Something should fit you. We can get you a toothbrush once we get to Milton," Solomon kept talking as he walked.

"I'm not wearing some girl's leftovers, Sol!" I tried to keep my composure while looking at my work in review.

"There are only three women allowed in my home, Three!" He obviously meant, Mrs. Montgomery, Angela, and me.

He had aunts and female cousins, but they were southern belles and often stayed below the Mason Dixon line. They often opted to stay in very elite resorts when traveling out of town. Mrs. Montgomery was more like me--practical. She loved her children and respected and supported her husband. Wherever her children or her husband went, she went. I did miss my relationship with her.

I went to the room on the right as instructed. It seemed like the furniture was never touched, except to be cleaned. Above the bed was another one of my paintings circa 2004. It was the most recent in his collection. It was called *The Crimson Door*--a signature piece I painted while finishing up my time at St. Augustine's. The installation featured all of the historical buildings on the yard and what would become the future of the college, a name change to a university under the leadership of the current president. At the center of the painting was the historic Episcopal Church. Highlighted were the red doors of the church's entrance. It symbolized salvation to those who entered them. I purposefully made it three-dimensional. It was the first painting that greeted me in his foyer. I sold this painting to an anonymous patron at Senator Duff's fundraiser when I graduated. Then, it hit me. That night was full of anomalies.

"Solomon, did you..." I let my words hang in the balance as I continued to scan the room for more artwork from that night to support Senator Duff's campaign for re-election. I pondered. "Did you write me a check for $6,792 at St. Augustine's in 2004?

CARAMEL'S SUNDAY

JPEG 019
The Reveal

Silence was the response to my question about the anonymous donation I received at St. Augustine's. I stepped out of the room to announce it again. This time, I repeated the question with my hands on my hip and eyes facing Solomon. Like Glenn Close's character in *Fatal Attraction,* I was not going to be ignored.

"Solomon, did you give me a check and a note at St. Augustine's in 2004 at Senator Duff's fundraiser?"

I guess I should have prepared myself for the possibility of Solomon changing his clothes. He turned around in nothing but his boxer briefs and a smile. I shyly turned around.

"It's okay. You've seen me like this before," he said in jest.

"I know, it's been a while, though. Now stop evading."

"I'm not evading. I'm just trying to figure out where you're coming from with your question. I'm clueless."

"In 2004, I introduced Senator Duff at her fundraiser at St. Augustine's. I saw a familiar person in the shadow, but couldn't make out the face. Later that evening, I received a note and a check for the balance of my tuition from an anonymous donor telling me to follow my dreams. Then, I come in here and see not one of the paintings, but several from that night on your walls. So, again, I ask, did you write me that check?"

Solomon paused, put on a pair of jeans, walked toward me with a smile, and said, "It wasn't me. I wasn't even there."

"Well, how in the world do you explain all the paintings from that night, and the rest of your shrine of my work?"

"First of all, I collect art. It just so happens that you're my favorite artist. You got a problem with that, shorty?"

Solomon hit me over the head with a pair of his balled up socks.

"Secondly, the paintings in that room were given to me by my..." Solomon paused.

"By your who?" I inquired further.

"Wait. Wait. Did you say the check was for the balance of your tuition?"

"Yes, I did." I twisted my neck a bit to seem firm in my unwavering colored-girl stance.

"Yo! Didn't you apply for the Ryland Greene Scholarship?"

"Yes! I did. I didn't get it though. My portfolio wasn't impressive enough, at the time."

Solomon sat down on a long, brown, leather ottoman, smiled, and chuckled a bit.

"I don't believe it." Solomon applied one sock then another. "He kept his word after all these years."

"Who? What word?" I sat beside Solomon on the ottoman.

"My dad," he said.

"Your dad? Why would your dad write me a check? Why would your dad be at St. Augustine's College? He doesn't believe HBCUs add value to a resume. I'm confused."

"You know I feel differently about Historically Black Colleges and Universities. Anyway, it's going to be a long ride up the road. I'll fill you in. Did you grab some clothes out of the room, Mel?"

"Uh! I didn't have time. I was too busy trying to make sure you weren't stalking me and preparing me for the remix of *Misery*," I said.

"C'mon, son! You know me betta than dat!"

"Alright, with your bogus New York accent. You

straight outta the south!" I punched him in the arm as I made my way back to the room with the promotional clothes.

Solomon was pretty busy over the years. The clothes were top brands. He had a closet full of men's and women's apparel, shoes included. I was really shocked to see women's lingerie with the tags still on them. I wasn't into lace, but I found a few pairs of boy shorts to fit my booty nicely and a sports bra to cup my size B just right. I didn't have much in the bosom department, but they were round enough to look full and nice in any shirt.

I didn't get a chance to see Ralph again because we headed to an underground parking garage from Solomon's apartment. He had two rides--the get-around car and the one he calls *Mr. Floss*.

Mr. Floss was a custom-made hard-top convertible in his favorite color, forest green. It was a graduation present from his father. The body was a BMW with top-of-the-line parts.

The chrome on the wheels was subtle. He preferred the matted look instead of the glossy-shine chrome that drew too much attention. The wood-grained interior was masterfully crafted. The dashboard had his initials carved in it--SMB.

CARAMEL'S SUNDAY

Mr. Floss, the car's name, didn't have a smell; it had an aroma of pine at all times. Solomon cleaned it, faithfully, every three days. Even if he was out of town, he paid a car service to handle the routine cleaning and or dusting in his absence. As Solomon said, "It's a luxury I can afford." He believed in keeping his investments up so he wouldn't have to go to the trouble of buying replacements. My engagement ring was no different. I was expected to get a thorough cleaning or buffed at least twice a month. Although it wasn't a diamond, it was still an investment.

The tank was full; we just had to place our things in the trunk and get on the road. I was anxious to hear about the check from Mr. Montgomery. He never thought I was good enough for Solomon because my financial and social pedigree didn't come close to the Montgomery way of life. Still, he respected Solomon's decision and was cordial toward me. There was only one time I gave him the side-eye. At Solomon's college graduation party, he invited Melissa Francis, a girl Solomon escorted at a debutante ball. They had a brief fling together, but Solomon wasn't stuck on her. She wanted to lose her virginity to him the night of the ball. He tried to talk her out of it, but she insisted if it was going to be anyone, it should be him. Solomon recounted the night as being the one moment when he knew just how powerful money could be.

"Money is so possessing that it convinced a good girl to give up her goods just to say she let the bank roll up in her." She didn't want the relationship, but the claim to say he was the first. Nevertheless, Solomon's dad would bring up Melissa at least once each time we gathered for a meal and I was present. It was a bit rude, but I wasn't concerned. I understood the song and dance.

Mr. Montgomery loved that Melissa's father owned quite a bit of commercial real estate in the South and was planning to expand north and west. A Montgomery and Francis union would prove beneficial for all parties involved. Solomon didn't care one way or the other, but he did pull his dad to the side and had a *word* with him. I never spoke of it, but I remember seeing him get firm with his father in a tucked-away part of their mansion. I wasn't trying to get involved, but I knew what was happening the moment Solomon spotted Melissa--who was as smart as she was beautiful; however, the party was the last time we saw or heard about Melissa. Solomon didn't make her leave, but I didn't see her much more after he spoke with his dad.

CARAMEL'S SUNDAY

The first 30 minutes of our ride included a full explanation of an agreement Solomon made with Mr. Montgomery before coming to Gaston High School. Essentially, if Solomon received a scholarship that could have otherwise gone to a student who couldn't afford to pay for college, Mr. Montgomery would use the money from Solomon's trust fund to pay for his or her education. Solomon did, in fact, receive the Ryland Greene Scholarship. It was the only one that was not need-based and he was eligible to win.

Solomon had a strong engineering, music, management, and marketing background. No one in the state of North Carolina could match him. I certainly didn't have the resources to compete, at that time, to be multi-faceted in my craft. I, apparently, was the recipient of the Solomon Montgomery Trust Fund Scholarship. What I didn't understand was Mr. Montgomery's attendance at St. Augustine's College.

"So, my dad is a big supporter of Senator Duff. They became friends after meeting each other on a retreat while they were both in college."

"How did their paths cross? Your dad's circle is with the elite--the Harvards, the Yales, the Amhersts..."

"The MITs, etcetera, etcetera. I know. I know, but what you didn't know is that Senator Duff was Dad's high school sweetheart," Solomon glanced at me quickly.

"Hold up? What? But...how? And what does any of this have to do with the check he wrote to me?" I was so very confused.

"I'm not even supposed to talk about this, but I started now," Solomon said.

"Yeh! You sorta hafta now!" All rules of proper speech was left somewhere between Solomon's apartment, Lenox Avenue, and the turn onto the exit leading to the George Washington Bridge.

"Okay. How can I put this?"

"Don't put it any kind of way except to just say it," I pleaded. He was right, this was going to be a very long ride. I had begun to put my camera in the back seat so I wouldn't get distracted by the sights and sounds around me.

"Dad and Senator Duff are kinda like you and me. Senator Duff comes from modest means and Dad was sort of like a wealthy you."

"What are you trying to say?"

"I'm saying, the Brooks family empire had no influence in the Duff household's view of him. No matter how long the Brooks dollar was, Senator Duff's dad wanted better for his daughter; he wanted Senator Duff to be with a hard working man who would love and care for her only."

"...but Senator Duff never married."

"Now you know why..."

"Wait. Are you telling me she and your dad were an item?"

"Sort of but not really."

"How so?" I asked further.

"Grandpa Brooks wouldn't agree to let Dad see anyone outside of the family circle. So, Senator Duff always remained as Dad's classmate who occasionally made cameo appearances. She impressed Grandpa Brooks with her ability to negotiate and organize community leaders to rebuild under-resourced areas in North Carolina. Doing so, gave Grandpa Brooks inside scoops on revitalized areas that could benefit from distribution centers for Brooks Foods.

"I tell you, the men in your family stay thinking about profits. Again...how does what you said to your father connect to you having my paintings?"

There was a pause. Solomon reached for my hand. I started to resist his grasp, but I relished in the warmth of it.

"Dad finally realized that you were my Senator Duff. Your artwork was his way of apologizing. He figured he owed me."

What could I possibly say? I never, in a million light years, would have guessed Mr. Montgomery would ever give Solomon his blessing.

"What made him come around?

"I made him remember his love for Senator Duff," Solomon said.

"...but what about your mom? Does he love her or..."

"There's no *or*. He loves my mom. He grew to love her more when she acknowledged that she understood the ways of the affluent and she promised to spend the rest of her life supporting whatever he needed to honor his family's name and business. Please know that Mom Dukes did not have a shortage of suitors either, but she, too, made a decision."

"Wow! I guess love in the old days came with sacrifice."

"I think all love does. The greatest of loves came with the greatest of sacrifices," Solomon said while pointing upward. Solomon was never a truly religious person, but with the passing of time, someone might have shown him the light of Jesus.

Without sounding totally oblivious to God's word, I threw in a heartfelt *Amen*.

"You do what you have to do with the information that you know. He needed to be reminded of his bones. I wasn't going down like that."

"Explain, sir."

"I want what I want. How about that!"

"...and when you don't get what you want?" I released my hand from Solomon's embrace.

"Well, I haven't had a chance to experience that yet, Mel Caramel."

"Man! Keep driving."

We came up on the ramp for Interstate 287. The rocky side of the state of New York was coming into view. There was so much more to the Brooks Family now that I no longer had a shallow view of their history. In fact, all of what had been happening in the course of three days was coming into focus. I wasn't sure what would come of my time with Solomon, but it cleared up some things for me. Solomon put me ahead of his family's tradition even when I didn't know it. Maybe his hustle was simply to make a new family tradition, and not so much to put me to the side intentionally. I would keep watch. We still had time to chill on the facts.

My phone rang and I answered it without notice.

"Hello, there, miss. Do you know who this is?"

"Uh...yeh, of course."

"Tell me then."

I paused and looked at Solomon grinning with one hand on the steering wheel and leaning slightly to the side toward me.

"Mr. Banks."

Solomon's grin was now accompanied by a side-eye and a straightened posture. I was sure his ears were pointed too...like the tip of a radar.

CARAMEL'S SUNDAY

JPEG 020
Cha Ching!

Jeffrey Banks was truly tenacious. While he was on business, he wanted to make sure I had him on my mind. I was so into Solomon's story about his father's skeletons that I failed to screen my call. I wasn't trying to hide anything, but it was rude of me to pick up. I blamed it on my reflexes.

After getting off the phone with Jeffrey, I tried to avoid possible questions about the call, so I started asking questions about Solomon's last visit home, but Solomon wasn't having it.

"So, what's up with my man, J. Banks.?" he asked.

"Huh? Who? Mr. Banks?"

"Are you always that formal with him?"

"Why do you want to know?" I asked.

"Why aren't you answering the question, woman?" Solomon teased.

"Well, Mr. Banks...I mean Jeffrey is helping me develop my business. That's why I was at the fundraiser the night we ran into each other," I said.

"You were there to develop your business?"

"Sort of. I was networking. He gave me an invitation he was supposedly no longer using."

"I see." Solomon didn't seem convinced. I don't know why it mattered whether or not he believed me, but it did.

"You see what?" I probed.

"He got you a ticket so he could sit next to you to cop a feel."

"What? No! Huh? What are you insinuating?" I punched Solomon in the arm playfully.

"Mmm hmmm! I saw you girl. Giving up that thigh. He probably invited us to his house in *Morewood* to sniff me out. I had his niece, and he wanted to make sure I didn't have you, too."

"Whatever, man. Why would he care?"

"Mel? C'mon. You're playing, right?"

"No! Really. I'm serious."

I did know what he meant; I just played the fool. I wanted to hear Solomon's thoughts before interjecting my own. The more he talked, the less I had to reveal about Jeffrey and me--which really wasn't much, but we were having such a good time catching up that I didn't want unnecessary drama to enter the atmosphere.

"Okay. So how long have you known dude?"

"Hmm...a hot minute."

"A hot minute, huh? Define that minute, Mel," Solomon asserted.

"I dunno. Let's see. I met him last year and we just reconnected a little while ago."

"So a stranger..."

"He's not a stranger, Sol!"

"Oh! My bad, your lover..."

"...not my lover either, silly. Now you *c'mon!* If you didn't get a taste of the Caramel, some dude I met about a year ago ain't gonna get a scoop."

"So you admit it, he is some dude!" Solomon got excited.

"Wait! What I meant to say was that I didn't give up my cookie." I was able to quickly regain my composure. Solomon set me up for the bait.

"Okay! Okay! So, my man, Jeffrey, is just dishing out expensive ass tickets to a woman he barely knows is what you're saying--with no strings attached?"

"I guess so. He seemed really interested in helping me launch my next business venture."

Solomon whispered, "That ain't all he's interested in helping you do."

"Well, my legs aren't open for business. I'm too busy trying to keep my eyes on the prize."

"That's good to know," Solomon said.

"What's it worth to you anyway?"

"Hey, I've known him a little longer than you. He's cool, but he enjoys the company of pretty ladies. When he's set on one in particular, he does what's necessary to keep her. I'm just trying to look out for my girl."

The way Solomon said *girl* was comforting. I knew he did not mean any ill will my way. Solomon might have been probing for information about who I was dating, but at the beginning of the day, he would want me to be careful about the company I keep as friends. I'm sure he's seen quite a few girls ruin their life's ambitions because of bad choices in relationships. I would, however, hope he would give me more credit than to sell my golden treasure to the highest bidder. I was just as focused in my present as I was in my past. Besides, it would have been crazy for me to open up the magic between my legs to someone I barely knew.

The ride to Milton took a little more than two hours. There was an accident on the Interstate. We were able to pull over to a diner off the beaten path called Charley's. We were starving. Charley's was a hole in the wall, but it was just right for our existing hunger needs. Traditional American food was the fare. I was tired of burgers and fries, so I opted for the slow cooked pot roast and mashed potatoes with baby carrots and pearl onions. If the cook with the tattoo fit any stereotype, I certainly hoped it was that he could cook really well and had a fresh-baked apple pie to accompany my meal.

I secretly liked diner food because I knew my meal was made to order--or so I hoped. Solomon ordered the chicken pot pie with a side of broccoli. He was longing for comfort food on a plate instead of a plastic container. This was a great segue back to an earlier question.

"So, you never really answered my question about going back to Garysburg."

"I haven't been back to North Carolina since..." Solomon pondered.

"It's been that long, huh?"

"Yeh! Probably since you broke up with me through email."

I grew silent. Solomon tried to break the awkward thickness in the air with a quick laugh to let me know his comment wasn't personal.

"I'm just messing with you, Mel, but I really haven't been home since then. I've just been meeting Mom and Dad on location during their travels," he said.

"Oh! 'Cause I was about to say..."

"Say what?" Solomon dared.

I twisted my neck toward Solomon and lowered my eyes at him.

"I was about to say..." I never made it to whatever I was going to say before Solomon slid out of his seat, sat next to me, and stared me in my eyes.

"What, Mel? What were you going to say?"

I stared back in a sort of paralyzed state. By the fifth blink of my eyes, Solomon planted a kiss right on my lips. I didn't resist. I couldn't resist. I was warm inside and out. The only thing I could hear was my heart beat and the neon lights from the open sign of the diner. It was steady. *Buzz! Blink! Blink! Buzz! Blink! Blink!* Then, without notice, a bit of a drip let loose in my panties. This time, I knew for sure it was not my period. Solomon Montgomery Brooks turned me into a dripping faucet.

What seemed like an eternity was just a minute. I know because the clock on my cell phone had only jumped one number since I last looked at it on the table. That was a powerful minute. Solomon released his wet lips from mine, licked them, and then wiped a new smile on his face with his hands.

"I'm not going to apologize for that kiss," he said.

"I wasn't going to ask for an apology," I responded.

"I wanted to kiss you the first moment I saw you in that dress in D.C. I missed you, Mel."

There was nothing for me to say. I had no words. I did what came naturally. I kissed his lips. We were now even, but I felt like a loose cannon. With that impulse, I remembered just how tasty kissing Solomon was. His breath was a song beckoning me to come home to fresh pine trees. It stayed minty fresh from mints and chewing gum all day.

Another powerful minute passed, then I managed to say, "I'm glad I'm here."

"Good. Me, too," he said.

"Me, three! Now scoot your boots back over to the other side, son, so I can feed y'all!" The server with the name tag *La La* interrupted our grown folks after school special.

We regrouped as La La placed hot buttered rolls on the table.

"I brought y'all some water to cool you off a bit," La La said.

We laughed with La La. It was a little too late to try and play off our public display of affection. It happened. It wasn't raunchy, I suspect, but it was visible to other patrons. The guy sitting across from us gave Solomon an *OK* wink. The lady walking past me shot up two thumbs. The server was more like a mom. She gave us some advice.

CARAMEL'S SUNDAY

"If y'all ain't married, wait. Ya hear me? I know what I'm talkin' 'bout."

Her thick southern accent was noticeable. She was definitely not from any part of New York I had ever traveled. She was homegrown below the Mason Dixon Line--it was clear. Nevertheless, I'm glad she was our officiate to remind us about waiting. For a moment, I almost forgot my virtue. For a moment, my life's camera was out of focus. While I never had intercourse, there was something in me that wanted Solomon to be my main course.

CARAMEL'S SUNDAY

JPEG 021
Friday Eve

The Sweetest Suite Cake Company
www.thesweetestsuitecakecompany.vpweb.com

CARAMEL'S SUNDAY

Milton, New York was everything Solomon said it would be. It was located in an area called the Hudson Valley. Way up in the mountains, the tree-lined roads welcomed us with open arms. I felt like I was in the scene in *The Wizard of Oz* where the trees came to life. Instead of throwing apples, they would give new meaning to tree hugger. There was, however, one thing I quickly learned about Milton: the place was not without a shortage of apple orchards. There were plenty of signs where you could get your pick of the *Finest Apples Ever Grown,* as one orchard noted on its sign.

Night had fallen, but I could see Earth's debut before me from the headlights shining on it. I couldn't wait until day break to take out my camera and start shooting. There was too much natural foliage and animal life for me to keep my camera inside its case. I had the bright idea to create a new work to my E.Y.E. portfolio--A Taste of the World. I would first start with the New England. I was happy to have found my mojo beyond the kiss in the diner. I was back on my grind and for a moment, I forgot that Solomon was still in the car. A force field of beauty surrounded me.

"So what's the plan when we get to your friend's house?" I asked.

"You know, I never thought I would say this, but I'm actually tired. We've been up since the crack of dawn," Solomon said with sincerity.

"This is true," I agreed.

With all the excitement from the day, my adrenaline was high. I had forgotten that we started out with an early train ride to New York City for an afternoon of shooting. While photography might not look like work, it can be mentally and physically exhausting. Then there was the emotional discussion about my artwork and the great reveal of my anonymous donation at St. Augustine's in 2004. The world turned at the diner when Solomon and I shared our second first kiss after years of separation. He was right, it would be *beddy-bye* time once we arrived to the house. I would not be averse to a hot bath, a cup of hot tea, and a long, deep sleep.

"Do we have to stop and get groceries?" I asked.

"You know. I didn't think of that," Solomon said slyly.

I let his comment linger, and for once, just sat back to enjoy the rest of the ride. After all, he did say that he had things covered. I would think less of him if our meals weren't planned. When we arrived at our destination, a ranch-style brick home was nestled in the woods behind a gate. An attendant greeted us. It was clear that Solomon covered everything. He surely had a kind friend who let us post up at the last minute.

"You know I don't need all this," I reminded Solomon.

"I know. The butler just comes with the house." Solomon giggled and then popped the trunk from the inside of his car.

"I guess the butler will get my things," I asked Solomon.

"Nope! I got it. Go in and have your tea. I know what time it is." Solomon ushered me inside. The butler held the door open for me. Solomon knew me too well; he remembered that I enjoy a cup of green tea before going to bed.

The rest of my stay in Milton was peaceful and all about me. I awoke to a note with Solomon's car keys.

Eat breakfast and explore the town. A map is in the car. Meet me back at the house at 3 or sooner. Have fun.
-Solomon

I was up at sunrise so I didn't need the whole day

to take in the sights and sounds of Milton. I needed to capture its beginning and its ending. I loved the solitude, but I didn't want to waste time being too selfish. Solomon had taken time to spend with me and rebuild our friendship, so I made sure I carved out some more catch up time.

My Thursday morning was filled with Bambi, Rocky, and mountain ranges that screamed, "Take a picture of me!" So I did. I didn't have to travel far from the house because everything I needed to capture was within a 10-mile radius. I picked up a maple-glazed, apple bacon scone from a local coffee and pastry shop called Suites and Thais. I stayed long enough to make a new friend--the owner Patrice Jackson.

I told her I was a professional photographer, and she shared with me that she always wanted to be a photographer. Her love for coffee and baked goods trumped her photography ambitions. We connected, and Patrice sent me on my way with a fresh loaf of cinnamon raisin bread and her special homemade honey butter.

By noon, I had seen all there was to see to capture my surroundings. The people varied in shapes and colors. If there were any race related problems, I didn't witness any because men and women were coupled up without regard to ethnic background.

Everyone smiled with peace as mixed-raced lovers embraced one another.

The stores did not lack variety. Instead of being inundated with athletic or department stores, Milton and Poughkeepsie offered their residents specialty stores for yawn, bikes, books that that highlighted local authors as the stars, and bakeries that actually baked bread and pastries on site. A bakery's smell cannot be manufactured. It is created with flour, sugar, butter, flavor, and love.

Biking and running were the chosen recreation for the early part of the day for families, couples, and singles alike. I even ran into a man who was bird watching. He let me disturb him for a moment just to get his name and information so I could call and talk about his passion at a later time.

I had experienced the wonders of Upstate New York and was a positively overwhelmed. The remainder of my day was spent cutting the fool with Solomon. There was no pressure to be intimate. Solomon and I just talked, laughed, picked a few apples from the trees in the back yard, and let Mr. Baker, the cook, use us as guinea pigs for all meals made with the apples. For dinner, Mr. Baker made turkey apple turnovers accompanied by an apple walnut salad served with apple vinaigrette dressing. For dessert, we had Dutch apple pie. It was nice to make a mess we didn't have to clean up, but we helped anyway. We weren't children, so the least we could do was take our dishes to the kitchen sink.

After dinner, I gave full disclosure on the nature of my relationship with Jeffrey--how we met, further explanation about the thigh incident at the fundraiser, and that I might have some interest in Jeffrey Banks. I also told him about my pending dinner with Jeffrey as well. Solomon wasn't the least bit surprised or unsettled about my interaction with Jeffrey.

"It's natural. I'd think something was wrong with you if you had no interest in anyone. The last thing I want for you is to be sitting around looking at a litter of kittens to buy on the Internet," Solomon joked.

"I don't even like cats, Sol," I replied.

"I'm just saying. Just 'cause you got the cat on lock doesn't mean you shouldn't date...even if the lucky dude isn't me. Be happy, Mel, is all I'm saying."

CARAMEL'S SUNDAY

Solomon was always calm and cool about things. His confidence made him attractive. He cared, in his way, about the things he loved. He was, however, determined not to let too much in life get the best of him. He had his own money and access to a family empire, but his happiness and the happiness of others meant more. His pride dwelled in a greater quality of life not the quantity of things he could acquire.

Because I didn't want to be too tired for my trip to Garysburg on Sunday, I asked Solomon if we could head back to Maryland early in the morning. I also wanted a buffer day before my dinner with Jeffrey on Monday. I wanted to at least give him a fair shot at a pleasurable dinner. Solomon certainly warmed me up quite well.

We spent the rest of the evening looking over my business plan--I had my laptop with me. Overall, Solomon was impressed with what Shelly and I worked on and added a few more line items and details. When meeting with Jeffrey, I could be a bit more prepared; I wouldn't look like a lost puppy hanging on a thread because of lack of knowledge or research. My business game had stepped up a bit because my inner circle had increased.

CARAMEL'S SUNDAY

The alarm clock was set for three a.m., but I couldn't sleep. I pulled my phone out and turned it on. It had been shut off since Jeffrey's last call. I had 11 missed text messages. Five messages were from Dolly; she was being nosy. Four were from Shelly; she was being nosy because Dolly called her about my little vacay with Solomon. One was from Mr. Freeman asking me about my availability for a promotional shoot at the Largo, Maryland barbershop. The last one came from Miss E. It confused me.

Miss E.
I'm still with Sarah and Rebecca in the Caribbean. I'll be back in two weeks. My father is ill. I need you to meet me in North Carolina when I return. I'll text you with details later, Sugar.

There was very little I knew about Miss E.'s family except that she loved her sister, Sarah, and daughter, Rebecca, dearly. There was the history lesson she gave me about her running away with Sarah because she got pregnant and her parents didn't want her to keep the baby. I knew her family had some prestige because they owned some farm land. Other than those details, there wasn't much reason for me to be in North Carolina during her father's recovery except to give her a ride back home.

CARAMEL'S SUNDAY

Miss E.'s message was enough for me to lay my head down. I was looking at the back of my eye lids in no time. A previous dream was seemingly set on pause until I was in deep sleep. Solomon and Jeffrey picked up where they left off when I drifted off to sleep in Dolly's car. They were both reaching for my heart. I turned and ran into a field of tulips near familiar train tracks. The tulips transformed into cotton when I tripped. Gentle, tender hands raised me from the ground in the field. When I opened my eyes, a new face appeared. It was neither Solomon nor Jeffrey.

My vision was still a blur. I just knew that I was safe. A man cupped my head, carefully, in the palm of the his hands. My feet dangled like a child who had fallen off a swing in a sandbox.

"Sweet pea, only one of them could love you with the heart of a courageous man. Choose wisely," he said.

I wiped my eyes to see more clearly. The man was one of the seasoned citizens I had read to and swapped stories with at the senior center in Garysburg. He told me about his travels while in the military, and I shared my adventures while on photo shoots. I looked over his shoulder as Solomon and Jeffrey kept running toward me with their hands reaching for me with great fervor. I just looked back at the man and replied in an angelic voice, "Okay, Carl."

CARAMEL'S SUNDAY

JPEG 022
Expression and Truth are Freedom.

Solomon was right about Jeffrey. He knew how to get what he wanted. I don't think there's a word to adequately describe how ambitious Jeffrey could be to woo a girl. Yet, between both Solomon and Jeffrey, I saved a lot of money on gas. My purple Neon was at rest, on vacation, and enjoyed being in park because neither of them wanted me to go through the trouble of driving or getting where I needed to go.

On a pre-date conversation with Jeffrey, I explained how I would be running back and forth to North Carolina to volunteer at the senior center in Garysburg. Additionally, Miss E. needed me to meet her someplace for some reason--details were still pending. Jeffrey didn't want me to have an excuse to cancel our date, so he had his driver pick me up in Garysburg to bring me back to Fort Washington, Maryland. Once I was home, Jeffrey would have a driver waiting on me for whatever transportation I needed for the week until I could pick up my car in Garysburg.

"Jeffrey, I'm a big girl. The drive isn't that bad," I made my best attempt to convince him that the first-class treatment wasn't necessary.

"I'm sure you are, Miss Moss, but I have one shot to impress you. I'm not about to mess it up," Jeffrey said.

"Mr. Banks, you'll soon find out what impresses me. Throwing around money and conveniences are nice gestures, but I am a lot simpler than you think," I said.

I wasn't going to look a gift horse in the mouth. I told him his driver could pick me up at my Aunt Maggs's house. Then I requested he get me a rental for the week. I refused to have someone drive me around all week when my legs and arms were in perfect condition. Besides, Dolly would be getting married that upcoming Saturday. I didn't just have points A and B to travel; I was traveling from points A through Z on a time clock that didn't exist. He agreed to the rental, and I thanked him.

Our date took many interesting turns. Jeffrey picked me up from my apartment in a limousine. He stepped out in a pair of jeans, a white shirt, and leather shoes. It was the most casual I had ever seen him. He wasn't kidding when he encouraged me to dress comfortably. I told him comfort is what I do best. He asked me what I felt like eating. I told him I wasn't in the mood for anything fancy. I just wanted some pizza--

knowing that my dough was being tossed in the air made me happy; I love fresh ingredients. I didn't mind waiting for quality. Just because I may have seemed like a cheap date, my taste didn't have to suffer for it.

Jeffrey looked at me in silence with his hand on his chin, then he said, "I think I might know the place." Jeffrey tapped on the window of the limo and said a few words to the driver. Then he opened up a compartment and passed me a packaged bowl of fruit.

"It's going to take us a while to get where we're going. Eat up. I don't want you to starve."

I was curious, but didn't bother to ask. If Jeffrey was a dangerous person, Solomon would have told me; so I, once again, learned to enjoy the ride.

It seemed we both had the same sense of humor and liked some of the same movies. We popped in *Coming to America* starring Eddie Murphy and couldn't resist the quotable moments. We sang the hook to *Soul Glo* and fell out laughing at all the scenes when Prince Hakeem missed the mark on American culture. The fruit had long been gobbled up with both of us reaching our hands in the bowl at the same time. His hands were as soft as mine but still had the presence of strength and power.

Just before the two-hour mark in the ride, I noticed we were boarding a ferry. We were in West Virginia.

"This must be some really good pizza," I said.

"It is. You'll thank me later," he said and then grabbed the back of my hand for a kiss.

I gave him the side-eye. "Not in the way you think, but I hear you."

"I told you, Miss Moss. I am a patient man."

"We'll see about that."

The ferry carried us across the water. I imagined Jeffrey plotting to take us to a juke joint for dancing and pizza. Given our slight age difference, it was possible we'd have an old-school shake-a-leg kind of date. I was, however, mistaken. The limo eased off the platform and made three rights. The last right was down an arch-way headed in the direction of a vineyard. We were having Italian wine and pizza for dinner at Gregorio's. With the success of his movies, Gregorio invested in the food and beverage industries. I was slightly overwhelmed, in a good way, with Jeffrey's attempt to start my heart pumping by bringing together the connections from the first time we met with our present.

"You're going to love the pizza here. In fact, you get to pick out your own vegetables in the garden."

CARAMEL'S SUNDAY

"So it's my fault if I don't like the meal, and I can't ask for a refund?" I asked as we were being let out of the limo.

"I never thought of it that way, but I guess you're right," Jeffrey agreed.

The ambiance was beautiful and fragrant. It was dusk, so the lights around the vineyard were lit. Upon entering the restaurant, I first noticed the exposed brick with a splash of ocean blue paint. This has been Gregorio's signature setting in many of his films. He said it reminds him of days when he first visited Italy. There was brick and water everywhere.

The staff greeted us with smiles and welcomes. The smell of spring vegetables danced in my nostrils. The sharp smell of an array of cheeses intensified my hunger. I wasn't much of a wine drinker, but I was very curious about its taste straight from a vineyard. I imagine wine tasting bittersweet--like apple cider vinegar, but sweeter.

We were immediately taken to our table. Joining us was a basket of warm, buttered rolls. I remembered La La and Patrice from my dining experiences in New York.

"Are you sure you just want pizza?"

Jeffrey waved a roll just under my nose. I lunged

forward and took a bite. I was pretty quick, and it was pretty tasty. I wasted no time to snatch it playfully from Jeffrey's grasp.

"Feisty, are we?"

I chewed and then swallowed my piece of bread before saying, "It's more like I'm starving. That picnic basket of fruit wasn't going to cut it. I'm a country girl. Feed me, Jeffrey."

"Okay! Okay! I see you."

We looked through the menus in silence. I knew Jeffrey was hungry too. He was just playing it cool. He offered to order for me. I respectfully declined. While I appreciated the offer, I didn't want to feel like an invalid. He had already taken care of my transportation for the week. I was still cleansing from Solomon's spoil-a-thon, so I didn't want to overdose on luxury. I had to stay grounded and on task.

"So what will it be, ma'am?" The server gave me a smile and waited for me to respond. I ordered the mozzarella fritta and an Italian salad to start. For my entrée, I ordered the veal Florentine. Jeffrey was quite surprised by my tastes.

"You don't strike me as a veal woman," he chimed in while I ordered.

"I'm full of surprises," I informed Jeffrey.

Because I did say I wanted pizza, Jeffrey ordered one along with his regular meal.

"We want pepperoni, sausage, ham, and pineapple on it! Make it a large," he said.

"We? We're going to burst wide open eating all that food, Mr. Banks," I said.

"Whatever we don't eat, we'll split and take home," Jeffrey suggested.

I agreed. I didn't care how much money he made, I wasn't about to waste food when people were hungry.

After we finalized our order, a server escorted us back through the garden so we could pick our veggies for our salads and entrées. In addition to movies, there was one thing Jeffrey and I completely had in common at the table, we enjoyed food. His appetite, however, was a lot healthier than my own.

I rather enjoyed walking through the garden with Jeffrey. The air was still crisp even though the night had fallen. It wasn't balmy, it was just perfect. I wore my hair down, so the slight wind blew strands in my face. Jeffrey made sure to use his fingers to move them out of my eyes.

"So, tell me about you and Solomon Brooks."

A nice stroll did make for a peaceful time to inquire about my suitor--well, potential suitor in

Jeffrey's eyes. I was cautious about exposing all my cards about my past with Solomon. I didn't want things to get messy, but I was well within my right to date whom I wanted. I wasn't sleeping around with either of them, but from what I know about men, their egos are as sensitive as a woman's heart. I did my best to tread as lightly as I could without being deceptive.

"We were best friends in high school, became college sweethearts, and now we're friends." Truthfully, we were *hey I missed you, so let me kiss you* type of friends. That's what I agreed to tell myself.

Jeffrey just gave me an *Mmm hmm.* I expected a little more, but he seemed to be pondering and making chess moves in his head as we selected our toppings at the salad bar.

The salad bar was like a buffet, but the vegetables and fixings--minus the meat--were still in whole and raw form. We picked our carrots and they were cut or shaved to our liking. The leaves of our lettuce were peeled off the head. The tomatoes were still whole; the olives still had pits; the garlic was still in cloves, and so forth and so on. With all the wholesome food before us, Jeffrey's hunger was still not satisfied because my explanation about me and Solomon was still in pieces.

In between our vegetables being chopped and diced, Jeffrey continued with his interrogation.

"Now define college sweethearts. Does that mean you were in-love or just *kicking it?*"

Expression and truth are freedom. Because Jeffrey asked, I laid out my entire truth hand on the table.

"If love is getting engaged after Solomon graduated from Dukem, then there was love between two best friends who were going to spend the rest of their lives together."

"A Dukem man. Interesting. So, what happened?" Jeffrey really listened intently.

Our basket of salad fixings and entre vegetables were full bloom. The salad bartender handed them over to another server for the chef to prepare our meals.

"I broke up with him because I felt like I was being put in a box," I said.

"Wait! Wait! What? Please explain, Miss Moss." Jeffrey was amused and confused at the same time.

"What's this piece of Caramel history worth to you, Mr. Banks?"

To my surprise, he grabbed my hand and guided me back to the dining room.

"I think it's worth all my time to listen. I asked, so I am all ears."

Exposure is freedom. Jeffrey had the background information on the chronicles of Solomon and Caramel. Instead of feeling threatened, he looked at the history lesson as something he didn't want to repeat. His only comment was that we were young and that our youth teaches us to make better choices as we get older. In fact, he was glad I had the experience so I could further enjoy what it felt like to just be free--void of pressures.

"There is one thing you won't have to worry about me, Miss Moss. I want you to be exactly who you are. Don't change a thing about your creativity, loveliness, or ambitions."

"I hear what you're saying, but one thing you'll know about me is that I'm a woman of action, not words. You can save that for writers," I warned.

As he talked all I could hear is, *Aw yeah! Aw yeah! You know, life is all about expression. You only live once and you're not coming back. So express yourself. Yeh!* Salt-N-Pepa never failed me in a moment that could have potentially sucked me into a fantasy-land of seduction.

Jeffrey's strong arms and moistened lips were desirable, yet I wanted to be clear that my lady plumbing was not up for sale for good conversation and a delicious, fresh meal at Gregorio's. He almost had me believing with the hand-sliding along my shoulders and subliminal whispers in my ear that he was serious about waiting for me. Solomon had already warmed me up and warned me to stay the course.

After Jeffrey's attempts to get to me once he found out the competition existed, I tagged in to grill Jeffrey about who he was. Let him tell the story. He didn't have children and was not dating anyone because he stayed too busy to get serious. I questioned his outing with me. He responded that he made time for a potential investment. I served him a side-eye and twisted lip. He assured me that his intentions were honest. I went with it because that's the Spades hand he was playing. There was no reason to renege and lose books.

We switched to his love for revitalized areas. Jeffrey's *I pulled myself up by the bootstrap* story was the background to his *why*. He made investments in communities that needed empowering because someone invested in his dreams as a child.

"Being a product of a single-parent household is no big deal. It's pretty common these days, but caring for your single mom who suffered from lupus as you served as the primary bread-winner for four at the age of twelve was a different story," Jeffrey shared.

The man who gave him his start in business as a young apprentice was the same man who invested, dollar for dollar, every scholarship award Jeffrey earned to attend both undergraduate and graduate schools. By the time he entered his doctoral program, Jeffrey's education was 100 percent free.

"Horace Man said it best, 'Education is the great equalizer.' So I share my knowledge with communities that need a boost. In turn, I work with financial institutions to help small business owners in revitalized communities match, dollar for dollar, the investments the owners make toward their goals."

The rest of the dinner picked up where our ride left off--more laughter, more quotable lines, and a cornucopia of food. I didn't have any room for the tiramisu Jeffrey ordered, so we had it boxed for carry out.

The trip home did not serve either of us well. Our full bellies became sleep aids. I felt comfortable enough to doze off and woke up with my head on his shoulder.

"Wake up, Picasso. You're home." Jeffrey tapped me to wake up.

CARAMEL'S SUNDAY

I was a bit loopy and felt like my breath game was off--garlic, onions, and olives were in a boxing match inside my mouth.

"Ew! Oh, my goodness...!" I said out loud.

"No worries, I have the same taste in my mouth." Jeffrey handed me an mint. This move reminded me of Solomon. I let out a little gasp without clarification. It would have been rude to explain my action.

Jeffrey motioned for the driver to stay seated. He opened the door to let me out. He then escorted me to my door.

"*This bud of love, by summer's ripening breath, may prove a beauteous flower when next we meet,*"

"Shakespeare? That's how you close out the night, sir?"

"Is there any other way, madam?" Jeffrey responded to my question with a question.

Jeffrey pulled my hand toward his lips to kiss it.

"Good night, sweet lady. Next time we meet, it will be all about the Benjamins. In the meantime, I'll keep my E.Y.E. on you from afar."

CARAMEL'S SUNDAY

JPEG 023
How did I get here?

Of all the available women in D.C. dying to be with a powerful man, I don't know why Jeffrey wanted a creative artist who was constantly on the grind. I moved faster than his stocks. He seemed to enjoy the chase because I didn't pressure him to meet me at the altar. While he was appropriately given the last name Banks, his obvious wealth didn't excite me like other women. Even still, I refused to believe I was the only woman in his life. I was, however, the one who was real with my intentions. I played with a full deck of cards and showed every one whenever I was asked to show them. There were no hidden spades coming out to cut his heart. Because of my openness, I earned his respect and patience.

We met up in the middle of the week to review my business plan. He was impressed. I asked if he would still be impressed if I told him Solomon helped me.

"Money is green. I don't have time for envy. Now let's get this money," was his only response.

Jeffrey wanted me to submit the plan to one of the banks financing new businesses in Anacostia. There was an art space opening near *The Big Chair*. Jeffrey thought I should consider leasing space above or beside it before investing in a larger space. The overhead, he suggested, would bankrupt me.

"I want you to be in business for the long haul, establish yourself as a reputable art dealer, and then franchise online," he encouraged me to think larger than my personal ambitions. Long-term investments made dollars and cents to me.

After wrapping up, Jeffrey planned to take me to see the projected site for the arts center after grabbing some fish at Morton's. There were no places to sit in the mom-and-pop joint, but Jeffrey was fine sitting on the curb with me. I liked that he was grounded.

All plans were rolling well until Ms. Nunu hurriedly burst through the door to tell Jeffrey his two o'clock appointment was waiting for him. By the time Ms. Nunu could get out her words, a woman in red stood in front of the office door.

"Ready, baby?" the woman said in a very elated, high-pitched voice.

I couldn't put my finger on why she looked so familiar until I saw the diamond bracelet shining on her wrist. It was Rachelle Knox from the *Capital Offense* movie premier.

"See! I told you I'd wear my favorite piece you got me."

Jeffrey didn't miss a beat. He didn't seem shocked, off-balance, or anything.

"Yes! Dear. So you did. I was just finishing up with Miss Moss and her business plan. Rachelle Knox, Caramel Moss. Caramel, Rachelle Knox."

I extended my hand to shake hers, but Rachelle extended her arms to hug me.

"It's nice to meet you. I hope my Jeffrey gave you some good advice and showed you a new way to approach your plan."

"He did, actually." I cut my eyes at Jeffrey with a smile. He smiled back, shyly. That one encounter let me know that as smooth and brilliant as Jeffrey was, he missed a beat on this one moment. Crossing plans with two women was sloppy. I would expect that from a 20-something-year-old, not one who was knocking on 50.

"Mr. Banks. Thanks for the advice. I can manage the tour at the art space on my own. Just text me the address and put in a call to whomever is renovating the building."

"Of course, Miss Moss. Of Course."

I did extend my hand to Jeffrey. He extended his, but with a rub on the back of my hand from his thumb. There were no tingles from me. Focus is a wonderful thing. I don't like being caught off-guard. Play the books you claim. No one has time for *possibles* when your spades game and name are on the line. If you have 13 books, play your 13 books. If you're going board, go board and shut up. That was my thinking.

I was cool about it. As the universe continued to spin, my week carried on. Dolly called me while I walked to the rental. She wanted to give me the heads-up that she researched Solomon's company and sent him a last-minute invitation to the wedding by email.

"I always liked him for you, Mel," she said with the voice of a thousand plotting angels.

"I'm sure, but I'll be too busy getting the candid shots to entertain company," I told her.

"I know, but you need to enjoy yourself, too. So, let me initiate that without you bursting a vein, fathead."

"Whatever, cuz." I paused for a hot second. Then curiosity set in. I cleared my throat.

"...but what did he say?"

"It was an honest, innocent attempt, but he didn't reply. I just wanted you to know in case it came up in conversation. I know how you are about full disclosure on things."

Her timing couldn't be more perfect. I wasn't upset with Jeffrey; I was more disappointed that he had not revealed to me his other pursuits or conquests. The details of who, what, when, where, and why didn't concern me. Knowing *that* they existed helped me make better, more informed decisions.

I obviously missed the hint at dinner in West Virginia. He asked me if Solomon and I had seen each other after the fundraiser. I told him that we spent a week catching up and forgiving the past so we could be friends again. He didn't inquire much about any intimate moments. He just asked me if Solomon had intentions of seeing me more. I was honest and said that it wasn't up for discussion or an expectation. He was just being my friend.

"Well, did you know he and Tonya were an item at one time?"

"No. I didn't ask, but I'm sure if I did, he'd tell me the truth. It is all I require. I can't get past a lie too well."

The moment I said that, Jeffrey just simply bobbed his head up and down in agreement. I totally missed the chance to dig more into his life. The food had me off my game. It really was that good.

Additional getting-to-know-Caramel on a more intimate level, that was closed like a shutter. Helping Caramel push her agenda for a successful business was as open as a dilated iris. That would be wide open, and I would see just how far he could stretch his patience. I had other ventures that needed my attention. Keeping closed legs helped me keep my focus. I'll be honest, he *might* have had a chance to get close enough to smell it, as Shelly would always say, just so I could have some experience. Then I thought of Aunt Maggs.

"Honey, when you play with fire, you get burned." That was good enough advice. I have a low tolerance for pain.

I went to the art space on Martin Luther King, Jr. Avenue. I don't know how I missed it. Morton's was literally right across the street from the art space. The construction workers were heavily concentrating on blueprints yet to be built. I interrupted the work flow to ask for the foreman. One of the men in overalls and a yellow hat pointed to his right and said, "...the woman in the blue hat carrying the walkie talkie. Ms. Linda." I was mistaken. I needed to speak with the forewoman.

"Ms. Linda, hi, I'm Caramel Moss. Did Jeffrey Banks contact you about my arrival?"

"One minute, dear." Ms. Linda was a middle aged, black woman handling business. I had never seen a woman, let alone a black woman on site as the person in charge before. I heard about women entering more non-traditional leadership roles in business, but I was never that close and personal with one. It was very refreshing. It was black history month in the spring.

"Yes! Ms. Moss. Welcome. Nice to meet you. Please sign this release form, and then put on a hat and mask. One of my men will show you the space."

She was focused, cut, and dry, but still professional. The release form exempted Clarkson, the development company, from any possible mishaps. I was held completely responsible for myself. In other words, I had to enter the construction site at my own risk. I had to be careful and was on my own if I stepped on a nail, walked into a wall, or whatever. I made my visit very quick.

One of Linda's men approached me and showed me the space. It was a good thing I had vision. The building had not been remolded, but the space above the art center would be 900 square-feet total. It was small, but it would be completely open space. I could work with that. I wanted to consult Dolly to see what would be the best leasing rate for the space; I certainly planned to negotiate the price. Because my neighborhood connection was slightly compromised, I had to do some research on my own.

CARAMEL'S SUNDAY

I thanked Linda, returned the protective gear, and got ready for my next appointment with Mr. Freeman, which would take me about 45 minutes with traffic. School was just getting out and it was rush hour. The stop and go of carpools would delay my travel, but I set my time to meet him at six p.m. Lead time in D.C. was necessary. Anything could go wrong when making it from one side of the city to the next.

Given the day, I pumped the radio nice and loud with the windows rolled up. Oddly enough, it was so club-like in my car that I remembered I had a bachelorette party to attend--Dolly's. I would be late, but I was going to show up and have myself a good time.

All was set with Freeman's Barbershop. I had a shoot with his staff on Thursday morning. Thursday afternoon, I scheduled a manicure and pedicure so my hands and feet would be ready for the wedding.
Although I was going to be in my comfy black slacks and white top, I still wanted to make sure I wasn't going to look like I was kicking rocks with my hands and sifting flour with my feet.

It was a long Wednesday, quite the same as my Wednesday a week prior with Solomon, but it certainly provided me with more clarity. I began to switch off the ringer to my cell phone when I noticed I had three text messages to come in--one from Solomon, one from Jeffrey, one from Miss E. I checked Jeffrey's first, because it would only take a second to respond--if at all.

Jeffrey
Hey, sorry about that today. Let's follow-up on your visit next week.

Me
Sure.

He wasted no time getting back to me.

Jeffrey
Keep the car for the rest of the week. Have a safe trip back to Garysburg.

Me
Okay. Thanks, Mr. Banks.

I am sure he wanted more from me. I was sure that was all he would get at this time. I needed to be on my pints and quarts If I were to make Dolly's day special.

It was all about her and not about me. She was my muse for the rest of the week.

Next, I checked Miss E.'s note. Hers was a little lengthier than I expected. She wrote that she was the only one able to get back in the states. Something was wrong with Sarah's visa, and Rebecca didn't want to leave her aunt in Jamaica alone. They encouraged Miss E. to travel back home to take care of logistics for the patriarch of the family.

She also sent me the address where she wanted me to meet her on Sunday. I glanced at it. It was in Garysburg. I didn't understand. She told me things were complicated, but she wanted me to be there at three p.m. It was urgent. I responded with a simple, *I will be there.* That apparently was enough because she texted me, "Okay, Sugar. See you then."

I took a long shower before opening Solomon's text. I wanted to be as relaxed as possible to read whatever he had to say. I pinned my hair up into a bun, slapped a shower cap on, blasted my Brandy CD from freshman year at St. Augustine's, and enjoyed a 20 minutes to myself. In that moment, I realized that after 26 years, I still wore my mom's amethyst necklace.

I showered with it, slept in it, worked in it, and only took it off if it gravely interrupted my fashion-- wearing pearl earrings and a gold necklace was not a good look, even for me. I held the stone dangling between my breasts in my hand. Its energy gave me peace. There was solace and tranquility all around me. The music blasted, but it beat on an invisible force field while I zoned out thinking of my mom, the crazy few weeks, and all decisions I ever made since I was 16. It dawned on me, I was going to turn 30 in a few months. I accumulated a lot of memories that I could be proud to share.

Taking time out to reflect, I decided, was what I needed to do at least once a week. Wednesdays would have to be that day. There were too many voices trying to steer me, and I needed to make sure my voice was above anyone else's.

I dried off, moisturized with lemongrass body butter, and slipped on a pair of boy shorts and a t-shirt. My lady parts needed a moment, too. I was refreshed and ready to read Solomon's text while drinking a cup of tea.

Solomon
Your cousin invited me to the wedding. Do you mind if I come?

Me
Sure. You can stay with me.

Solomon
No need. I'm already in town. See you on Saturday.

CARAMEL'S SUNDAY

JPEG 024
She Did and Me Too...
(The Marriage of Love)

Sponsorship Provided by
Andrea Green Events and Designs
www.andreagreenevents.com

"Heads shots only, Caramel, until I get in the dress," Cousin Dolly whispered to me as she slipped on her pantyhose. I had always admired her beauty the moment she stepped on the gravel in Garysburg, North Carolina, in our youth. Her ponytails with pink ribbons were now traded in for perfect spiral locks bouncing from each side of her face. The rest of her hair was pinned tightly to form the healthiest mane I'd seen on a bride since I established my photography company.

I'm Violet "Caramel" Moss, Cousin of Dolly (Moss) Hunter and a long list of other Moss women in Northampton County, North Carolina. I was honored that Dolly trusted me to capture the intimate moments before her wedding. Before she became Mrs. Gerald A. Washington, Dolly trusted me with her last moments as a single woman to be caught between the shutter and flashes of my high-performance camera.

"Sistah, where Mama's pearls at? We can't let her walk that aisle without the famalee pearls." Aunt Maggs's blossoming eyes motioned for Cousin Sistah Rose to rush and get the pearls that traveled from Snellville, Georgia.

Snap! Flash! Snap! Flash! Dolly's angelic eyes

sparkled like stars as she turned to smile with her hair moving in chorus with the clicks of the camera. Snap! Flash! Cousin Sistah Rose bowed on one knee to present the box of pearls to Aunt Maggs. Snap! Flash! The matriarchs of the family encircled Dolly as is customary for every Moss bride when she marries her true love.

As Aunt Maggs placed the pearls around Dolly's neck as the Moss women started singing the song they created to the tune of *Oh My Darling, Clementine*:

She's a lady, a Moss lady
Who gathers to and fro
You are God's Chosen
Before you came here
That's why he loves you so.

The Moss women, although they have assumed new last names when married, continued to adorn Dolly with her something new and blue. The pearls served as both borrowed and old. I learned, in that moment, with the humming and communal tears why the Moss women saved this tradition for those who were truly in love. It was sort of a family blessing before the minister placed his hands upon the couple. The bride had to be covered in the love of those who came before her and made their marriages successful. It was a service packed with scripture, song, and the Holy Spirit. We all felt it.

I was the only single woman in the room allowed because this would be the first time it was caught on camera. Snap! Snap! Flash!

Just when the singing stopped, we heard a gentle knock on the door. It was the coordinator, Ms. Fannie.

"Ladies, it's showtime," she said.

"I'm ready," Dolly responded.

Aunt Maggs passed the veil to Dolly's mom. Our bride was ready to walk into her future with the blessing from a generation of Moss women.

Dolly ordered me to enjoy the wedding ceremony. In fact, I was not allowed to capture any moments during the service. It was asking a lot, but Dolly had her reasons. I left the bridal chambers and headed to the sanctuary. I was careful to hold the railing. The steps were steep, so I didn't want to make any scenes. Dolly was the show-stopper. No one needed to tend to me on account of my missing a step.

At the bottom of the steps was my best friend. Solomon had made it. He was as fresh of a sight to see as the baby's breath sprouting out of the hostesses' corsages.

"I thought for sure you'd be a bridesmaid, Mel."

Solomon extended a hand to help me down the last step. I accepted it.

"Naw! I'm not cut like that. You know me. Always in the background," I responded as we walked to the door to wait for a seating assignment.

"Did she at least ask?"

"Of course she asked. I told her I didn't need to feel that important. So, she kept things simple with her girls Erica and Cita."

"So simple, yet so kind."

"Always. There is less to apologize for later. I like it like that."

The hosts were my younger cousins from Garysburg. Even though we were family, they did not forget their duties. Rather than ask us which side to sit on, we were simply escorted.

"You sure you want me to sit with you and the family?" Solomon asked.

"I wouldn't have it any other way."

I was reminded to turn off my cell phone. I wasn't expecting any calls because I wrapped up things with Mr. Freeman. I hadn't heard from Jeffrey since Wednesday night. He was likely too busy to reach out because he was with Rachelle. I didn't care, but I sort of did. Nevertheless, I had my best friend with me. All was well in my world.

The ceremony was as traditional as most weddings. There was singing. There was scripture reading. What I wasn't prepared for was the mini sermon during communion. Half way through the minister's explanation on why we have communion, I noticed that I was rubbing my amethyst skittishly. It took Solomon to place his hands over my own to get me to stop rubbing it.

He leaned over to whisper, "Are you okay?"

I was experiencing something without knowing it. It was joy and grief all at the same time. The minister talked about the greatest love involved a great sacrifice. To give your life for the ones you love, which is greater than riches. It is greater than fame. It is greater than the wildest dream you could ever imagine. The minister reminded us of God's sacrifice for us--His followers, His children. I flashed to my parents and how their lives sang for me even in their deaths. Their love was undying when they encouraged me to try whatever made me happy. I just so happened to pick up the trades they loved. Some 22 years later, I sat in a seat and for the first time gave thanks to God for the gift of their love. Silent tears flowed. They felt thick as blood, and I didn't mind if they were.

Solomon just held me close. He didn't ask. He didn't need to; he knew my heart. With the world on mute around me, all I remember hearing was an invitation for me to give my life to Christ.

"Is there one?" the minister asked.

I stood. I had given my life to my dreams all these years, but on this day--a day I was to cheer on my favorite cousin as she wed her first love--I was to give my life to Christ.

"Now you know love," Solomon said.

He walked down the aisle with me. I looked and saw hands in praise and hands clapping toward me. A small crowd of church deacons and deaconesses surrounded me and others--including Dolly's best friend, Erica--in prayers and chants.

"Is there another?" I heard the minister ask again. More joined me. The wedding became a moment to witness love in its totality, at its root, and at its core. I was, ironically, in the middle of it.

In the crowd were several people who had played a major role in my life since my parents died. Aunt Maggs, Dolly, Uncle Jupiter, and even Solomon. I saw love, and I believed, without a shadow of a doubt, I was truly treasured--not out of sympathy or pity, I just was.

CARAMEL'S SUNDAY

JPEG 025
A Sundae on a Saturday

D olly was right to invite Solomon. If nothing else, having him at the reception eased the mind of some of my not-so-close cousins. They were almost sure I had become a lesbian because I broke up with *Solomon's fine tail,* and didn't seriously date anyone but my camera. Most of them were married with a starting line-up of children. It worked for them and their journey. I just wasn't there. The idea, however, wasn't so outrageous to me, but I wasn't convinced that was God's next step for me--now that my mind was even clearer.

Solomon and I danced and joked about who was going to catch the bouquet. Many of the single women on the dance floor looked so very thirsty to catch the bundled arrangement. I didn't dare go out there. I cared to keep my pedicure looking decent. When I get my toes done, I never aim to have them messed up until about week two. I'm not a girly-girl, but I do not believe in wasting money.

Solomon did, however, make his way to the crowd of gentlemen to catch the garter. Instead of men moving away once it was flung into the air, aside from Solomon staying stationary, the men scuffled for it. It was likely because my cousin, Tammy, the hottest thing since hot wings were invented, caught the bouquet. She was our pink sheep--she did not fit the mold of a Moss woman. She had a bit of a reputation, but her beauty could start and stop a war all at once. She was physically fit with a body that made any woman jealous.

We had a great time at the reception, but decided to escape for a bit to spend a few hours alone. So, Solomon and I decided to get some ice cream from the Dairy Queen after the reception. I had to bring him up to speed on Jeffrey Banks, who, by the way, finally called me just after my literal come-to-Jesus moment. We put his message on speaker while sharing a banana caramel sundae. We were like two middle school students sneaking to listen to messages from our teacher who shared a bad report.

Fortunately, the message was vague. Jeffrey decided to be smart and not sloppy this time. He simply shared that he had an opening the following week, and really wanted to keep his promise to support my efforts.

"You truly have the great potential to bring culture and the love of art to the Anacostia community. I want to be a part of that trend. I hope to hear from you soon," Jeffrey said.

Solomon didn't knock Jeffrey's hustle. In fact, he applauded him for keeping his promise.

"I'm not surprised. Mr. Banks is well connected. I don't doubt he wanted to get closer to you with honest intentions. Who wouldn't?"

"You're just being nice 'cause it's late and we've been connecting," I said after flicking a splash of water on his face.

"No, I mean it, Mel. I'm not trying to be funny when I say this, but both Banks and I can have our share of women. That's not a challenge. Most chicks..." I stopped him.

"Chicks, Solomon? C'mon. Your vocabulary is much richer than that," I encouraged him.

"My bad. My bad. Most women are looking for someone to sponsor them, take care of them for the rest of their lives. They want it all hocked up so they can just be comfortable without the work," he said.

"That comes with a price," I chimed in.

"Because you know that, and you have your own thing going, is why Mr. Banks likes you."

"Speaking of liking, did you and Tonya have a *thing?*"

"As a matter of fact, we did," Solomon didn't hesitate to answer. Three points! I knew my childhood friend wouldn't let me down.

"Hmm," I responded.

"Does that matter? Do you need to know the details?" Solomon asked with serious concern.

"Not really. I just wanted to see if you would tell me the truth."

"I'm sure Banks played that card to get a reaction out of you. If I know you like I do, you weren't fazed."

"Then you know me well."

"This, I do. Anyway, know that you're special. You've always been special down to your hermit ways to your still being a virgin," Solomon said.

"Is that weird, though? I'll be 30 this year, and I'm still a virgin."

"Jesus wouldn't think so. I don't think so--for selfish reasons, of course--but you have never worried about what others think of you. Why start now?"

"It was always funny when people asked if I was gay because I didn't have a steady boyfriend or if I needed to see a shrink because I never truly grieved the death of my parents. I guess I've been dancing..."

"To the click of your camera, Mel, Caramel."

"To the click of my camera. I'll take that, sir."

The rest of the night was casual. Solomon followed me home in my new rental. I had decided, after my meeting with Freeman, to turn in the rental under Jeffrey's name. Even though I was on a fixed income, I never wanted to be in a position where I owed anyone anything. Getting a rental in my name was the right thing to do. What I should have done was drive my little Neon back like I had the mind to do when Jeffrey first offered. It was a lesson learned. I was sure with more referrals I would make the money I spent back in no time.

I parked my car in front of my apartment building. Solomon parked beside me and then got out.

"I'm walking you to the door, so I'd appreciate it if you don't make a fuss about it," Solomon said.

"Are you sure you're not going to try and sneak your way into my place?" I joked.

"I'm not playing with one of God's finest. You just turned your life over to the Man of all men. You belong to Him now...until...forever."

Solomon's eyes were so very serious. I didn't have any reason to believe what he said wasn't true. I let him walk me to the door and forgot, in those few steps to the door, that Salt-N-Pepa had a song called *Independent*. Instead, the track in my head spun *Whatta Man: Here's to the future 'cuz we got through the past..*

We played the same hand in spades. On that night, I think if we had run a Boston in the game

Spades, we might have actually taken another team out--together.

CARAMEL'S SUNDAY

JPEG 026
Caramel's Sunday

"...the bottom line is that no matter how much control we think we have in our lives, God is in control of all things...Revelation is real..."

-Rachel West
New Carrollton, Maryland

Taking Exit 176 on I-95 is automatic for me. The green sign with reflecting white letters and numbers is always a magnet welcoming me to town, welcoming me home. As much as I love the scenes in the city, there was nothing like my roots in the country. The smell of the fresh scent of pine was Garysburg's perfume. Even the familiar smell from the paper mill still made me yearn to be closer to a kitchen, any kitchen, in Garysburg. Stoves stayed hot.

The country road leading to my family's home always hugged my car. I turned down my stereo to pay respect to nature and the neighborhood. Sunday service was in session, but I was sure Mr. Denton was washing his prized Buick so the women could see it shining as they brought him a plate to eat. He acquired the land by the train tracks, killed my field of tulips, and grew cotton. Yes, cotton--the white stuff from which America profited off the backs of my black relatives. Mr. Denton rarely left the house so he could keep watch on the crops. He found a way to genetically manufacture it. Cotton usually blooms in the autumn, but Mr. Denton's operation was year-round. He had the cotton industry on lock in Garysburg.

CARAMEL'S SUNDAY

I waved to Mr. Denton. He waved, smiled, and went back to washing his Buick. He always let me take a moment to relish in the field's beauty because he remembered it was one of my favorite places to meditate as a child after the three o'clock train passed.

"New car?" he asked.

I rolled down the window to respond, "Rental."

"Awright, now! Good seein' you!"

"You, too, Mr. Denton."

"Carry on!"

The color of the cotton was white, but would transform, in my mind, into many different colors for many different purposes. Those cotton blossoms would welcome me home with waves from slight winds. Rather than scowling at the fluffy clouds, I smiled at the possibilities of what the field of dreams could become--a shirt for the first black president, a lab coat for the scientist who would find the cure for cancer, a dress for the first Native American woman to be sworn in as a Supreme Court Judge, or simply a pair of socks for the firefighter who saved the lives of many while risking his life in a fire. Wherever those little cotton blossoms found a home, I wanted to have my shutter ready for their debut.

CARAMEL'S SUNDAY

I parked the rental behind my car. Aunt Maggs had moved it to the gravel so she could get her car out for her sojourn north. I used the house keys to let myself in. Ordinarily, Aunt Maggs would have a hot meal waiting for me, but she was still in Maryland wrapping up details from Dolly's wedding. I wouldn't have the pleasure of seeing her sitting in her rocking chair on the porch or finding some way to escape her favorite question, "Have you found my nephew, yet?

I would smell her fish, grits, greens, and corn-bread as soon as I walked in the door. I would also smell the pressure of a generation of aunties when I hugged her. She would grab my hand after embracing me and ask, "Where's my nephew hiding?" It took me years to rehearse my reply: "God is working on him." This time, I would have said it and truly meant it.

My frustrations regarding the pressures of life relaxed at Dolly's wedding. When I crossed the imaginary crossroad in my life, I exhaled and saw that in order to receive all that my heart desired, I had to let go and know that not all journeys are meant for me to travel alone.

The senior center wasn't expecting me, but I thought to call to see if they needed any help before heading to the address Miss E. sent me. I didn't want to open up the text up completely so it would be the first thing I saw when looking at messages. Unfortunately, my services weren't needed, but Jack, the director, said I could come by if I just wanted to hang out.

"You're always welcome, here, Caramel," Jack said. I thought I'd take him up on the offer later. It was only 10 a.m. In the meantime, I took the time to chill at the house. I set my alarm clock for 2:30 in case I dozed off.

It is in quiet moments that you find yourself and see yourself more clearly. The silence wasn't as deafening as I would have imagined, but voids in my life began to fill, slowly but surely.

I flipped through the family photos and found pictures of myself when I was first born. The caption read, "Violet's First Day Home." I was a big, fat baby. Mom must have really gone heavy on the sweets while pregnant with me. There were pictures of us at Myrtle Beach. I was playing around with children of all races. It was my third birthday. I was building a toddler's version of a sand castle with some white girl with red hair. I looked more clearly. The white girl with red hair was me. I know it was me because of the amethyst necklace. It was strange. I never remembered being that light. I hadn't realized I had the necklace so long. I took a closer look at the picture and saw that the darker girl was Dolly. I guess when you sit still long enough to remain still you can hear and see more things in real time, in three-dimensions, and just see and hear with clarity. I just chalked it up to time--I caramelized a bit more as I got older.

I walked in the kitchen, even though everything in it was cold, to see if Aunt Maggs had some leftover anything. She didn't disappoint. There were two pieces of pound cake sitting in the bread box. I was winning. She must have baked the cake shortly before traveling for the wedding. The butter kept the cake moist. There was about a glass-full of milk left in the container. I killed it, but wrote a note to myself to replenish the jug. That was the house rule once I was old enough to have an income: *If you finish it, buy another one.*

I climbed the wooden steps to what was my room growing up that turned into a sewing room. After finishing St. Augustine's, I sent my degree to Aunt Maggs. She put it in the room to celebrate my success. She didn't want it in the general living area because she had too much company on a regular basis and she didn't want anything to happen to it. She also wanted me to remember the great work I accomplished over time.

CARAMEL'S SUNDAY

In the same room were my trophies, ribbons, and awards for art competitions I won throughout high school. I framed the rejection letter from the Ryland Greene Foundation to motivate me to keep pressing forward despite obstacles. I always said I would write the foundation to let them know I made a successful life for myself beyond their help. The older I got, the less that ambition was a priority. They had their criteria and selected whom they wanted. Now that I know Solomon was the recipient, it was money well spent on their end. I came out on top later. Things always have a way of working out.

The sandman bagged my eyes, and before I knew it, my alarm went off. It was time to freshen my breath and get ready for whatever Miss E. had planned for the afternoon. Still confused, I just prayed she didn't want me taking family photos of her ailing father. I would do it for her but I'd be holding my breath and wind up passing out at the end of the shoot.

I got in the car, flipped my phone--yes, I said flip; it was 2006. The address was to the senior center. Now I was quite sure there were not that many white seniors in the center. Those who were there did not bear the surname Hamilton. Peebles was Miss E.'s married name. There was Mr. Carpenter, a retired postal worker;

Ms. Piccadilly, a former cashier at the Piggly Wiggly; and Ms. Bleu, a blonde-haired blue-eyed woman who claimed to be from French royalty. I would just sit and listen to her for pure entertainment. The rest were black men and women who were either retired military or just simply didn't want to live with their children or other relatives as they got older.

I drove on looking for answers inside my head. I came up empty. Maybe Miss E.'s father traded in his farmer's plow for senior living and owned the building. Perhaps Miss E. is looking to move her mother in the senior center if her father died and she wanted me to work some magic to get a good rate. Maybe Miss E. liked my tales about Garysburg so much that she wanted to sell her property in Waldorf, Maryland and move back south to be closer to home. My moment of clarity was clouded. I remembered to center myself with thoughts about God's blessings in my life to balance the noise levels.

The center was just a few miles down the road, so the drive wasn't long. Jack was outside the center wheeling Ms. Bleu around for her afternoon stroll. She said she lost the operation of her limbs while running to save her lover from a hidden gunman during World War II. She slipped and fell upon seeing him being blown to pieces. It was the reason she decided to move to the United States. Her file, however, says that her real name is Blanche--still French-like--and she was in a really bad car accident. Her memory never fully recovered, nor did the circulation in her legs. She has since created a new life of her own. She is no danger to anyone, not even herself. She is just not living her reality.

"Hey, Jack!" I said.

"Caramel! It's always great to see you." Jack released the handles of Ms. Bleu's wheel chair to hug me. She about lost her mind until she realized it was me. She is somehow convinced we're related. The way she tells it, her great-grandfather owned slaves and brought them to America. He fell in love with one of the slaves. The baby of that union is my great-grandmother. We just went with it. If nothing else, her stories made for interesting shows on the History Channel. I was her favorite Negro niece. No matter how many times I had to correct her with the term, she was stuck in a time period.

Because most of my family was still away, I asked Jack if he would trail me to the car rental facility and drive me back to the house so I could get reacquainted with my vehicle after a week apart.

"If it's after five p.m., I am at your service my lady."

"Lady? Jack, I'm the only lady here," Ms. Bleu shouted with a forced French accent.

I looked at my watch. I had 10 minutes to kill. I told Jack a feisty, older white lady was to meet me at three p.m. and not to kick her out if she gets fussy. Instead, I gave him Miss E.'s name and asked him to escort her to the lobby to wait for me. I was going to give hugs to my crew in the cafeteria. It was game and snack time.

I was like a super star when I walked into the newly remodeled *mess hall,* as Mr. Carl called it. The residents of the senior center acknowledged with smiles, heavy waves, and a few *Heeey, Caramel* shout-outs. Ms. Piccadilly waved a bag of Golden Fish Chips to usher me to sit next to her. That was her bribe even though she knew I was more of an Oreo girl. Any bag of snacks, she thought, would give her an edge up on others competing for my attention.

"I don't know how long I can hold on to these fish, Caramel! Come see me soon," Ms. Piccadilly shouted. I just laughed.

Mr. Carl usually sat in the corner of the dining area playing checkers with Mr. Fred, another retired vet, during game time. Mr. Fred was playing with someone else that day. I sure hoped nothing happened to Mr. Carl. I inquired.

"Mr. Fred, where is Mr. Carl?"

"Aww, sweets, he's fixin' to leave this joint. His true love found him."

"Huh? I thought she died or something."

"Oh no! He just said he lost her after the war. Lost as in he couldn't find her anymore, but now she's back!"

"Wow! Well, I'm going to run to see if I can catch him. It sure won't be the same without him."

"It sure won't, but it's always great to see you. Come back soon, ya hear me?" Mr. Fred reached his one arm up for a hug. I squeezed him good.

I peeked in the lobby to see if Miss E. had arrived. She hadn't. The vending machine was on the way to Mr. Carl's room. I had a dollar in change. The cost for goods was low in the senior center because all the residents were on a fixed income. I was able to get both of us a pack of Oreo cookies for fifty cents each. It was a small going away gesture. I was going to miss my little buddy.

His eyes were once a chestnut brown, but over time, cataract, had made them slightly cloudy. I understood how his eyes worked because they were just like the lens of a camera. I was always very sensitive about his vision and made sure any book I brought him was in large print.

Mr. Carl was still a very young and handsome man, but time, surgeries, and lost love took away the elasticity from his face. He wasn't a drinker or a smoker; he never consumed recreational drugs. Life was just hard on him at 55; he looked more like he was 65 or older.

I tapped on Mr. Carl's door to announce my arrival.

"I have our cookies!" I said with a smile on my face.

To my surprise, sitting on Mr. Carl's bed was Miss E. She didn't wait to speak. She just clearly said the following words: "Caramel, this is your father."

CARAMEL'S SUNDAY

Dear Coffeedreamz family,

Thank you for taking this journey with Caramel. I am sure most of you are pretty lost, confused, and some of you might still be flipping the pages to see if you missed something. I have some good news, and I have some bad news. The bad news is that the story has ended, for this season. The good news is that the continuation of the story is already in progress.

For those of you who have been with me since 2001, you know I love to give you twists and turns. If you felt like you were in limbo with Miss E. 's last words in the book, you know how Caramel feels.

Caramel's Sunday was written for every person who felt a social or family pressure. It is about life, love, and finding balance even when you stand alone. *Caramel's Sunday* encourages you to stand your ground when your head is filled with everyone else's dreams and ambitions for you.

Caramel's Sunday also includes an elephant in the room--virginity. If you got caught up with the fact that Caramel is a virgin and find that *unnatural* for a healthy, almost 30-year old woman, consider it a metaphor. Purity is above and below the waist. It starts with our thinking. If our minds aren't clouded, we are less likely to make poor judgments. Will we make mistakes? Yes. It's called being human. How we respond to those mistakes is key. Getting upset, or as my middle school students say it, *TURNED UP*, does not get us closer to a resolution. Even though I created the character, Caramel taught me one thing during this project--pick your battles, but always keep things moving. I am interested, however, to see how she handles this next journey in her life.

Caramel's Sunday is personal to anyone who felt like answering Langston Hughes's question in his poem

CARAMEL'S SUNDAY

Harlem also known as *Dream Deferred. Caramel's Sunday* is personal if anyone had to go on the same quest as Janie Crawford in Zora Neale Hurston's *Their Eyes Were Watching God* to find out about love and living. *Caramel's Sunday* supports and encourages people with ambitions. Caramel and Solomon speak to readers who aspire to see their dreams without thirsting for wholeness in anything other than their faith and passion.

Both characters were created to help readers to see their goals through with the cookie cutter model as a guide and not the end product. Getting married and building a family are gifts; they do not define a person. Wholeness is also not defined by a clock or others' concepts of realities. There is a blessing in waiting. *Caramel's Sunday* invites readers--both male and female--to craft a reality that is tailored especially for them.

As I exhale and meditate on the next steps in Caramel's journey, I challenge you to begin thinking of what day of the week will be your moment of truth when all you can do is stand and wait. Be clear about what you want on a Monday, Tuesday, Wednesday, Thursday, Friday, Saturday, or Sunday. Create your soundtrack to life that will lead you. For Caramel, it was Salt-N-Pepa. For you, it might be another genre, singer, group, or rapper. Whatever breathes into your life, be firm and convicted by it no matter the noise around you. Silence naysayers and sing your songs.

Here is to your special day when your life takes a turn but you're still able to stand.

All the best,

Yolonda D. Coleman

www.yolondacoleman.com

About the Author

Yolonda D. Coleman was born, reared, and educated in Washington, D.C. Upon graduating from Benjamin Banneker High School, she attended Hampton University in Hampton, Virginia for her undergraduate degree and the University of Maryland University College for her graduate degree. Coleman's ambition was to be the next Oprah Winfrey as an on-air personality. Yet, she set out for a new stage--the classroom. Still, with an Oprah-like spirit, Coleman wrote poetry and devoted over a decade of her career to educating students in grades six through twelve as an English and communications teacher.

It was, however, in 2004 that two students who Coleman affectionately calls CIA and FBI said, "Quit teaching and write your book." It was on November 19, 2004 that Coleman stepped out of the classroom. By July 2005, the Sugar Rush series was born.

Sugar Rush: Love's Liberation is the first installation in the *Sugar Rush* series. The sequel, *Sugar Rush: Love's Elevation* became an amazon.com bestseller in three categories just seven days after its release. Caramel's Sunday is Coleman's fourth major project.

While Coleman has since re-entered the classroom, she does so while still writing and building more dreams with her husband in Maryland.

www.ingramcontent.com/pod-product-compliance
Lightning Source LLC
Chambersburg PA
CBHW031601240626
47153CB00002B/592